ACTION

ALSO BY DEAN WESLEY SMITH

COLD POKER GANG

Kill Game

Cold Call

Calling Dead

Bad Beat

Dead Hand

Freezeout

Ace High

Burn Card

Heads Up

Ring Game

Bottom Pair

Case Card

THE POKER BOY UNIVERSE

POKER BOY

The Slots of Saturn: A Poker Boy Novel

They're Back: A Poker Boy Short Novel

Luck Be Ladies: A Poker Boy Collection

Playing a Hunch: A Poker Boy Collection

A Poker Boy Christmas: A Poker Boy Collection

SEEDERS UNIVERSE

Dust and Kisses: A Seeders Universe Prequel Novel

Against Time

Sector Justice

Morning Song

The High Edge

Star Mist

Star Rain

Star Fall

Starburst

Rescue Two

ACTION

A Cold Poker Gang Collection

DEAN WESLEY SMITH

wmg
PUBLISHING

Action
Copyright © 2023 by Dean Wesley Smith
Published by WMG Publishing
Cover and layout copyright © 2023 by WMG Publishing
Cover design by Allyson Longueira/WMG Publishing
Cover art copyright © trybex/Depositphotos

ISBN-13 (trade paperback): 978-1-56146-874-4
ISBN-13 (hardcover): 978-1-56146-875-1

Due to limitations of space, expanded copyright information can be found on page 153.

CONTENTS

ACTION: A COLD POKER GANG COLLECTION

Introduction

I think *Action* is the best name for this collection for a few reasons.

First of all, these stories are mystery stories with action of varied levels. Just the nature of the beast with detectives and mysteries.

The second reason is the old cliché on how you start filming in a movie. "Lights! Camera! ACTION!" A number of the stories in this eight-story collection actually do start novels. Not all of them, but some of them.

I first mentioned the Cold Poker Gang in my thriller *Dead Money*. Sort of a toss-off comment in that book about a task force of retired Las Vegas detectives that met and played poker once a week and were sanctioned by the Chief of Police to solve cold cases.

I thought the idea so much fun that over the next few years I wrote more short stories featuring them and about four or five novels. I put them out under my own name, but since Dean Wesley Smith is considered a Star Trek and Men in Black writer, the mystery series got very little traction.

I honestly didn't care. I just kept having fun writing them and publishing them. Each book stands alone, just as each story in this collection does as well.

And for me, riding along with two experienced retired detectives solving cold cases was the most fun I could have sitting in front of a computer.

It wasn't until the ninth book that mystery readers discovered the series and it exploded. It seems there was a hunger for stories about retired older people falling in love and solving cold cases.

Selling a lot or selling a few, I write them because I have fun writing the stories. It actually made no difference to me.

Then in the fall of 2022, my wife gave me an assignment to write a holiday story for the Holiday Spectacular, a regular series of three anthologies she edits every year. The stories could be about any holiday and are sent out like an Advent calendar to all the subscribers every day from American Thanksgiving to January 1.

I thought it would be fun to write about the cold case of D.B. Cooper. (He hijacked a plane in 1971 and bailed out with a ton of money and was never seen again. Maybe the nation's most famous cold case.)

But I figured the story would be better as a Cold Poker Gang story and that story is in this collection, the very last one in the book.

But when I finished with the story, I could not get the setting and the idea out of my mind, so along came *Case Card*, the newest Cold Poker Gang novel.

You can see how I used and expanded and changed the short story to be the first numbers of chapters in the book if you get both this collection and the new *Case Card* novel.

"Lights! Camera! ACTION!"

A word about the eight stories in this collection. I decided to put them in the order I wrote them to also give you a sense of how the Cold Poker Gang Task Force evolved.

The introductions and cover from each story were in my magazine *Smith's Monthly* and the introduction to the last story is the introduction from *Holiday Spectacular*.

Over the years there have been a number of teams in the Cold Poker Gang Task Force, playing poker one night a week in Retired-Detective's Lott's basement and solving some of the most puzzling cold cases Las Vegas can throw at them.

Hope you enjoy the stories as much as I did creating and then solving them.

Dean Wesley Smith
Las Vegas, NV

DEAN WESLEY SMITH

THE CASE OF
THE PLEASANT HILLS MURDER

A Cold Poker Gang Story

Dean Wesley Smith introduces us for the first time to Retired-Detective Lott and the rest of the retired Las Vegas detectives who play poker, solve cold cases, and call themselves the Cold Poker Gang.

They solve cases every week, but this case becomes very personal for Retired-Detective Lott. More so than any cold case he and the Gang ever tackled before. And as with most cold cases, solutions do not come easy. And answers tend not to be what anyone hoped.

CHAPTER ONE

January, 1992
Pleasant Hills
Las Vegas, Nevada

The afternoon felt dark and gloomy, the wind kicking a chill through Nesto Poretz's gloved hands and light jacket as he expertly dug at the soft soil along the ridgeline with his backhoe, taking large shovelfuls of dirt quickly to one side and dumping them on a pile, then returning the big shovel for another in almost a seamless movement.

The sound of the engine a constant rumbling to him, something he was used to after all the years. Something that he sometimes missed at night, when his apartment was quiet, the kids asleep.

He loved the simple noise of a working machine. There was nothing better.

The sky was cloudy and threatening, coloring everything in the normally brown desert a dull gunmetal gray. Nesto's job, before it got dark, was to get as much of the foundation dug out for this new house as he could. He wouldn't get it all done, but enough to keep his boss happy.

Danny, a tall thin white kid stood beside the hole Nesto was digging, leaning against his shovel. Danny had far too much attitude and thought himself too good to be working this kind of job. He considered himself a real catch for any woman and loved to brag about his conquests, most of which Nesto was sure were completely made up.

For some reason the boss had hired the idiot and had assigned him to Nesto three days ago As far as Nesto was concerned, letting Danny stand and lean on his shovel was the best place for the kid. That way he didn't screw anything up.

Nesto dumped a shovelful and swung the shovel back over the hole when suddenly Danny shouted "Stop!"

Danny ignored the hand-signals Nesto had taught him and jumped down off the edge into the hole.

Nesto got the bucket stopped just in time, shaking his head and wondering if he would have just done the world a favor not getting the bucket stopped in time. But then he would have had to live with Danny's death and that kid just wasn't worth it.

Most of the time the kid wasn't worth the air he was breathing.

The hole was only about four feet deep where Danny had jumped down and then bent over, so Nesto couldn't see him.

Suddenly Danny scrambled up the bank and out of the hole faster than if some woman was chasing him for child support. He ran about ten steps, then bent over and threw up.

Nesto watched him for a moment from his seat on the rumbling back-hoe, then put the machine in reverse and backed away from the edge and shut the engine down.

The silence swarmed over him like a blanket as he climbed down. The cold wind tried to push him back from the foundation hole he had been digging, but he moved over and around to get a better look at what had caused Danny to lose his far-too-expensive lunch.

In his ten years working backhoe, Nesto had dug up a lot of things. Some not so pleasant.

From the looks of how Danny stood, his hands on his knees, shaking his head, this was going to be one of those times.

Nesto moved around and then finally, with a deep breath of the cold afternoon air, he looked down into the hole.

A man's head and left arm were there, sticking out of the dirt.

Most of the guy's skin was gone, his eyes blank sockets, but the guy's brown hair still clung in place.

And on the wrist was a fairly new watch.

Gold watch.

Nesto had just found his third body. The two before had been old settler's skeletons. This one was far from that.

He turned for his truck to call in to dispatch to get the police coming. There was no chance he was finishing this job tomorrow.

More than likely not even next week.

The boss was not going to be happy.

CHAPTER TWO

May 2014
Pleasant Hills
Las Vegas, Nevada

At six-thirty, I took two bowls of Lays chips down the half flight of stairs to my poker room. I had had the poker table custom built a year ago and sized it perfectly for the area to the left side of the staircase. It could seat eight, with eight matching brown leather chairs around the table. There was a place at each seat to hold chips and a drink and a comfortable light over the table.

I loved that table and felt at home sitting at it.

I already had the chips in place and an unopened decks of cards sitting on the wet bar beside the table. It was Tuesday night and I was flat excited for another fun night of poker with the gang.

I had decorated the rest of the room in framed posters of different Las Vegas events from the past, including one classic showing Sinatra and Martin. A large couch and two recliners filled one end of the room facing a large screen television.

I had to admit, I had spent far, far too much time in this room since my wife, Connie, died two years ago. That's why last year I had decided to completely remodel it and make it the perfect place for me to spend time.

I had made the room all mine, and Annie, my daughter, thought that was a great idea. Upstairs, for me, Connie was still there. I didn't mind that. I thought about her every day and still can't believe I managed to keep going after she died, But somehow I had, thanks to a lot of help from Annie. Now this basement was my space.

Three of the gang said they would be here tonight for the game. Sometimes we had six or seven on a Tuesday night. Most of the time we ended up with only four.

We called ourselves the "Cold Poker Gang" since we were all retired detectives and every Tuesday we played poker while we sat around and talked about cold cases.

I loved poker and I loved being a detective, so Tuesday night didn't come fast enough for me every week.

During the week, each of us would take a case and run down leads and bring the results back to the gang. Just as when we were on the force, one would take the lead on each case.

I just couldn't believe how much I looked forward to the game every week, and especially this week since the case I had lead on for the last month I had finally solved. Together, the gang had solved ten cold cases in just under a year and since we were working for free, that record of closures sure made the Benson, the Chief of Detectives, happy.

There was a loud knock at the door just as I sat the chips down on the bar. I glanced at the time.

Someone was very early.

I headed back up and got to the front door as the knock came again.

Retired Detective Andor Williams stood there, a file folder in his hand and a frown on his face. It was William's turn to get a new case from the city for tonight, for me to take lead on. The tradition was Williams would present the case to everyone during the game.

Williams looked the oldest of all of us, with almost no hair, wrinkled face, and sloppy clothes like an old man would wear. At seventy, he was still very spry and walked like he was always late for something.

Just like what had happened to me, Williams had lost his wife two years ago, and at times it seemed to me that the gang and solving cold cases was the only thing Williams went on living for. Both of William's kids lived in California and he seldom talked about them. He spent far more time than anyone working on his assigned case as well as helping others with their cases.

Williams said, "Lott, good seeing you." Then he handed the file to me, and pushed past. "Figured you needed to see this before we open it to the gang."

I stared at the file in my hand. It was an official homicide folder of the Las Vegas police, with the words "copy" stamped on both sides.

Normal.

I pushed the door closed and followed Williams to the staircase and back down into the poker room. Williams took his normal seat with his back to the staircase and I took the file and went to the wet bar and opened it, spreading it out on the marble top.

It took a moment for me to finally see what I needed to see and why Williams had brought the case to me early. A murder victim had been found in January 1992 and the case never solved.

"Holy shit!" I said.

"My opinion exactly," Williams said.

I was so stunned, I didn't know what else to say.

I just kept staring at the address where they had dug up the vic, not really believing it wasn't a joke or something. The body in this cold case had been found right here.

"That's why I brought it over early," Williams said. "They found the body when they were digging this very basement twenty-two years ago. Go figure, huh? And I can tell by the look on your face no one told you when you bought the house."

I had nothing I could say.

I had had no idea. And I was pretty darned certain Connie would have never agreed to buy the place if she had known.

This was now one of the strangest cold cases I had ever seen.

CHAPTER THREE

May 2014
Henderson
Outside of Las Vegas, Nevada

I banged on the weathered screen door on the small house, knocking some paint flecks loose. Beside me Williams stood, looking stern and official. Or at least as much as he could with his rumpled suit and unshaven face.

The weather was headed toward the warm side for the day, a promise of the hot summer to come. We were about two blocks off the old Boulder Highway, in a Henderson neighborhood that had seen a far better time in the past. The houses here were small and the yards tiny, built to house casino workers coming in during the first boom in the late 1960s.

The house we were at hadn't seen a coat of paint in a decade or more and the lawn had long since turned to weeds, only slightly green now because of the wet spring we had had.

I had no idea what we would find, but this was the address we got for the dead guy's daughter.

"Yeah," a woman's voice came from inside the house, then some rustling around and the door opened.

Both of us had our guns unstrapped and ready, just in case. If there was nothing else we had learned over the years, we didn't go knocking on a door without being ready for anything to come at us.

As the big, paint-peeling door swung open, the stench of uncleaned cat boxes and stale beer hit me, turning my stomach. It was a toxic mix and I hoped like hell she wasn't going to invite us inside.

Beside me, Williams short of shook his head at the odor, giving a slight cough.

Through the dirty screen on the door, I could see an extremely obese woman in what had been a blue bathrobe that had more stains than color. She had short hair that looked greasy and a tattoo on her neck that was as faded as her bathrobe.

"Detectives Bayard Lott and Andor Williams," I said. "We're looking for Karen Rafferty."

"You found her," the woman said. She sounded like she had smoked far, far too many cigarettes in her lifetime as well as eating far, far too much.

The Chief didn't mind us introducing ourselves as detectives as long as he didn't hear about it. With our track record of closing cold cases, he was willing to let us drop the "retired" part at times.

Williams and I both flashed our old badges as well to the woman who just looked dazed, more than likely on something even this early in the morning.

"What do you want?" she asked. "That kid of mine get into trouble again?"

"No," I said, "we're here about your father, Nixon Rafferty."

She actually seemed to take a step back from the door and her face twisted up into something so ugly, I couldn't imagine being around her for more than a few seconds.

She pulled her poor, abused robe even tighter across her large bulk and said in a very cold voice. "I don't want to ever think of that bastard again. Not ever. He ruined my life and killed my mother and my baby sister."

With that she slammed the door in our faces, sending paint chips flying into the air around us.

I looked at Williams, who just shrugged.

"More than we expected," Williams said as we turned away.

I could only smile as we headed back toward my brand new Jeep Grand Cherokee, a Christmas gift from Annie.

That response had been a lot more than I had expected. We had solved a lot of cases on a lot less.

Now at least we had something to go on.

CHAPTER FOUR

June 2014
Pleasant Hills
Las Vegas, Nevada

I tossed my ten-jack off-suit into the muck as a response to William's three-dollar raise and sat back in my leather chair. Williams usually played tight and when he raised, it was either a stone cold bluff, or he had decent cards. Ten-jack wasn't a good enough hand to test the bluff theory.

The Tuesday night game of the Cold Poker Gang had four retired detectives around the table in my basement game room. The game we always played was pure Texas Hold'em. The stakes were one-dollar small blind and two-dollar big blind with a max bet of five bucks. The worst I had gotten hurt one week was two hundred and my best night winnings had been around one hundred and fifty.

All four of us tonight were good poker players, but not professional level like my daughter, Annie, and her boyfriend, Doc Hill. They both made more money from the game than I ever wanted to think about.

All the players tonight had no real worry about money, so the stakes were good, but not enough to hurt any of us.

To my right sat Ben "The Sarge" Carson. He was a year younger than I was at sixty-two and was in the best shape of all of us since he spent so much time in a gym every day. He told us it was a great place to meet women. I tended to believe him.

He had gray hair cut perfectly, a smile that he said had cost him a fortune, and more money than any one person should have. He was the only heir to a major fortune. Except for a new sports car, he still lived as he had when on the force.

He got his nickname from being a Sergeant in the Army before retiring and becoming a cop. Over the years that I had known Sarge, the guy had gone through three wives and yet managed to have no children. Now we all kidded him about looking for wife four, but he always said no, he had too much money to risk another wife.

Outside of the game or working on a case, I never saw Sarge without a younger woman on his arm. Always a different one as well, so Sarge's plan of avoiding another commitment seemed to be working.

The fourth member of the night was Conklin. I wasn't even sure of his first name since in thirty years I had never heard Conklin called by any other name.

Conklin was the only us here tonight with a wife. She supported his poker and cold case hobby because "It got him out of her hair." He had a badly broken nose that hadn't healed right and looked smashed on his face, and he never seemed to smile, although he had a dry and biting sense of humor.

He was also the only one of us with an advanced college degree. He had gotten a night-class MBA years back when he had considered quitting the force to start a business. Conklin always amazed me with his ability with numbers.

Conklin called William's raise and since he was dealing the hand, burnt a card and put three up on the board, face up. My ten-jack would have been even weaker since the flop had come king, five, four, all off-suit.

Williams bet three dollars again and Conklin just shook his head and folded, passing the deck of cards to Sarge for the next deal.

"So, where does the Rafferty case stand?" Conklin asked, sitting back. Every night he was the one to sort of do an inventory of the cases they were working on.

"It's just laying there like a dead, stinking fish," I said, feeling disgusted.

Beside me Williams nodded.

"The daughter said that the vic had killed her mother and her sister," I said, "but the mother and younger sister both died a few years after Rafferty went missing, both from drug overdoses."

"We got no idea what she was talking about," Williams said.

I felt slightly angry that I had to agree with Williams. This case just seemed to be going nowhere.

We had looked through all of Rafferty's bills and debts and he seemed like a poor working slob that no one had paid any attention to.

"So no luck there," Conklin said. "But when I was coming in here tonight I noticed your view, Lott."

I glanced at my flat-nosed friend. "Yeah, one of the reasons Connie and I bought this place."

Conklin nodded. "Back when Rafferty was buried up here, why would someone bury a guy they had just shot on a hill with a view?"

I glanced over at Williams. "That's a question I never thought about. Why kill a guy and then give him a view like you care about him?"

"Family," Williams said, nodding. "Rafferty was a slight drinker, but had no gambling problems and no mob connections or any other crime record. So it goes back to family or a mistress."

"We need more on the wife and younger daughter," I said, nodding. Now I suddenly felt like I had a direction with the case again.

Sarge dealt, then as he put the deck down, he said simply. "Family. If it's not sex that gets a guy killed, it's family."

"Spoken like a guy with far too much experience in both," Williams said.

"You can never have too much experience in sex," Conklin said flatly, picking up his cards and studying them as we all laughed and agreed.

But I knew there was a lot of truth in what Sarge had said. And chances are if we were going to solve the murder of the guy who had been buried right were we were playing cards, I was going to have to dig deeper into the mother and younger daughter.

I tossed away my seven-ten off-suit and sat back, sipping on my Diet

Coke and thinking about the next step in the case as the others all called the blind and waited for the flop.

It didn't get any better for me than Tuesday night.

CHAPTER FIVE

June 2014
Martin Luther King Blvd
Las Vegas, Nevada

I had done all the searching I could online of records about the wife and the younger daughter of Rafferty. But some of the older records hadn't been loaded up to the online services, so I found myself once again downtown in the Clark County Records building, the smell of dust and cleaning solution filling the air like a musty perfume.

It felt like old home week. I couldn't begin to remember how many hours over the years before computers I had spent in this building digging through records.

I had called Williams and got him to join me, since I knew Williams loved the musty paper files and didn't trust the information on the computers. He was as old-school as they came. And sometimes that had paid off for us.

It took us about twenty minutes, but we eventually found the death certificates for both the daughter and the wife of Rafferty. Both had died of prescription drug overdoes, way before that problem was even considered a problem.

"Take a look at this," Williams said, pointing to a name of the doctor who prescribed the drug for the daughter.

I glanced at the name and then the credentials. It was a psychiatrist.

I quickly glanced at the wife's file, then nodded and slipped it over to Williams.

"Same doctor," I said, pulling out my iPad, another gift from Annie, and doing a quick search to see if the Doctor Harriet Bert was still alive. It was always a problem with cold cases, especially really old ones like this. People had a way of dying or moving out of state and making it damn hard to track.

"Alive, but retired," I said, feeling relieved as I jotted down her address. It was a house address off the strip near the university.

"A visit?" Williams asked, smiling and standing.

"A visit," I said, glancing at my watch. It was almost noon. We might actually have a chance of catching her.

It turned out she wasn't home, but had started teaching part time at the University, so we tracked her to her office on campus in one of the older buildings.

The day was growing hot and both of us were sweating when we reached the red-brick building from the parking lot.

I felt very much out of place walking down the narrow hallway toward her office as students passed us, giving us both odd looks.

"Guess not many old farts take classes here," Williams said.

"No, they think we are professors," I said.

"Yeah, us professors," Williams said, and laughed.

"Why not?" I asked, laughing as well. "We could teach kids a thing or two."

"And both of the things would be wrong and outdated," Williams said as we reached Harriet Bert's office door.

Shaking my head and trying to not laugh, I knocked and a woman's voice said we should come in.

I went in first to be met with a room full of books, floor-to-ceiling, with a matronly woman sitting behind a big, wooden desk. The place was fairly large and smelled of flowers and tea. Or a very flowery tea.

We introduced ourselves and Harriet Bert switched glasses and offered us the only two chairs facing her desk.

"We are investigating the murder of a man by the name of Nixon Rafferty," I said.

Bert looked puzzled for a moment, then said, "Excuse me for a moment."

She switched her glasses again, leaving the other pair hanging from a chain around her neck and turned to her computer. After a moment she finally nodded.

"Sorry, just had to refresh a failing memory," she said, turning back to us and again changing her glasses. "I didn't know Nixon Rafferty was killed. All I knew was that he vanished suddenly leaving his family behind. I treated all three of his family for a time."

"That's why we are here," Williams said. "Rafferty's body was dug up in 1992. He had been shot. The case was never solved."

"So you are trying to solve the cold case now?" she asked, nodding. "I like that. What can I do to help?"

"As you mentioned," I said, "you treated the entire family after the disappearance. Could you tell us when your treatment stopped?"

She nodded, switched out the glasses again and went back to her computer. Then she looked over her glasses at them. "I treated all three for over a year, working to help them get past his disappearance, but all three quit at the same time in January of 1992."

I glanced at Williams. I knew that couldn't be a coincidence. That was when the body was found.

"We would never ask you to break client confidentiality, doctor," I said, knowing I had to be very careful and walk a fine line. "But both the younger daughter and the mother died later that year from drug over-doses. The younger daughter first, then the mother. The older daughter is still alive. But on the two that are dead, is there anything you would feel comfortable telling us about."

Doctor Bert frowned and went back to studying her records. Then without looking at us she said, "I remember when they died. They had used a prescription I had given them while I was still treating them. It was no longer valid since they were no longer in my care, but they somehow made copies and altered it and filled it at a dozen different places. Police ended up shutting a few of those places down after that."

I said nothing.

She studied the record for a short time on her computer screen, then switching glasses, she turned back to us. "I can tell you that Nixon Rafferty was a pedophile. He abused his youngest daughter and the mother had huge guilt feelings about letting him do that because she discovered it and let it go on. I was doing my best to help the two that died get past that. Clearly I failed."

I nodded and stood. I knew we would get nothing more from Doctor Bert. But now some pieces were starting to fall into place.

We thanked the doctor for her time and headed through the crowds of young students to get to my car.

"Think the family did it?" Williams asked as we climbed in and I got the car started and the air conditioning going.

I nodded. "One of them did it, and I have a hunch which one."

"Youngest?" Williams asked.

"Youngest," I said, nodding. "Now, let's just figure out how to prove it."

CHAPTER SIX

June 2014
Pleasant Hills
Las Vegas, Nevada

I sat watching the rest of the Cold Poker Gang battle over a hand. All three of them were in and Williams ended up taking it when he hit a third king on the river.

That clearly disgusted both Sarge and Conklin.

"Okay," Conklin said turning to me, "after that stupidity, how does the Rafferty murder case go?"

"Solved and closed," I said. I bowed slightly as the other three applauded.

"Williams had a lot to do with this as well," I said.

"So lay it out," Conklin said as Sarge gathered the cards and started to shuffle.

I explained how Williams and I had tracked down the psychologist on the prescriptions and she had given us the information that Rafferty had been a pedophile.

"Family?" Conklin asked.

I nodded, "But we both figured the younger daughter killed Rafferty in the act. She would have been twelve when he died and was fourteen when his body was found when they dug this basement in 1992."

"Why in the act?" Sarge asked.

"The bullet went into his mouth," Williams said, "in an upward direction and exited out of the back of his head."

"So he was on his back," I said.

"So she shot him," Sarge said. "Then the fourteen-year-old sister and mother helped bury him up here on the hill."

Conklin nodded. "Thus the view."

"Exactly," I said.

"Just ugly," Sarge said, shaking his head. "A tragedy all the way around."

"That it was," I said. "A twelve year old girl killing her own father. Doesn't get much worse than that."

"Didn't the detectives back when they found the body in 1992 make a run at the family?" Sarge asked as he started to deal out the next hand.

"They did, but had no luck," I said. "The three family members all held to their story that he had just vanished one night walking to the store for smokes. They were a complete dead end and the detectives then had nothing at all to point to them, or anyone else for that matter."

"So how did you get the older live sister to come clean now, after all this time?" Conklin asked.

"Good old-fashioned blackmail," I said, smiling.

"She has a son who's in and out of jail," Williams said.

"We got dealt some perfect cards," I said, laughing. "At the moment the son was in jail for a minor drug bust, so when they hauled the older sister, his mother, in for questioning, the detectives told her that her son would serve twenty years on the drug charge unless she told them the truth about what happened to her father."

"And the chief went for that?" Sarge asked.

I had to admit, I had been stunned when I suggested the idea and he had agreed.

"He did," I said. "The kid would have been released in a day or so, but she didn't know that. It was a pure bluff."

"And she caved to that?"

"She did," I said. "Spilled every last detail like she had been waiting twenty-four years to tell someone."

"She had," Conklin said.

"So her younger sister killed her father for what he was doing to her," Sarge said, nodding.

"And when the body was found, the guilt just overwhelmed the poor young thing," Williams said. "She could make herself believe that her father was just gone without the body and the investigation. But not after a funeral."

"Killed herself a month after the body was found," I said, "and the mother did the same the next month."

"Wow," Sarge said as he finished dealing out the cards. "What kind of deal did the older sister get?"

I shrugged. "She'll spend some time in jail for a number of charges. Chances are it won't be many since she was a minor when it all happened. And maybe she can now get some real help."

"Always an optimist," Williams said, laughing at me.

I glanced down at a pair of jacks and nodded. "Sometimes I am."

I raised three dollars and only Williams called.

"Now who's an optimist?" I asked.

"Trust me," Williams said, "these cards have a thousand percent better chance of winning this hand then that poor woman has in coming out of that family mess even slightly healthy."

And with that, I sadly had to agree. Sometimes solving old cases had their downsides.

But I still felt like a cop and it was my job, and this poker group's job, to dig up the past and solve the cases.

And even when what we found showed a true dark side of human culture, solving the case felt great.

I sat back slightly and watched Sarge put a third jack on the flop.

And somehow I managed to not smile.

It didn't get any better for me than Tuesday night with the Cold Poker Gang.

DEAN WESLEY SMITH

A BAD DAY FOR THE DREAM

A Cold Poker Gang Story

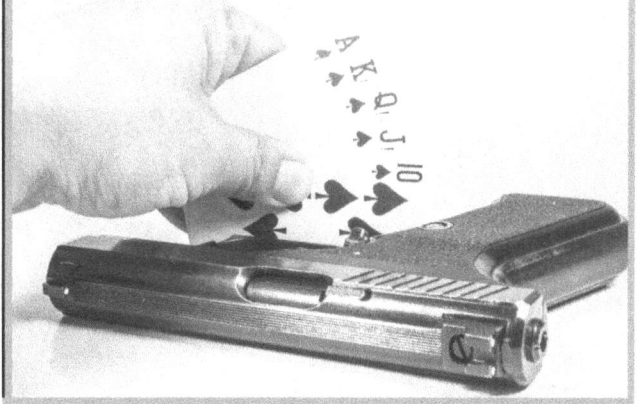

Thirty years ago in Las Vegas, Becky Penn said goodnight to her mother to go out with friends and vanished without a trace.

Retired Detectives Bayard Lott and Julia Rogers, members of the Cold Poker Gang, take on Becky Penn's cold case.

They love working with other retired detectives and playing a little poker once a week, all to solve cold cases.

A puzzle mystery unraveled carefully by the retired detectives who make up the Cold Poker Gang.

PROLOGUE

March 3rd, 1990
Las Vegas, Nevada

Becky Penn tied her long brown hair back away from her face and laughed as her mom stood in their bathroom door, arms crossed over her chest, the worried look that Becky saw so much from her.

Her mom had raised her since their father had left when Becky was three. The two of them were more like sisters at times and Becky loved that.

Becky was dressed in a light skirt, a new blouse she had just bought, and had on sandals, since the weather was already starting to warm up.

Becky's mom had already changed from her nursing scrubs into a light sweatshirt and jeans. She seldom wore shoes around the house and tonight was no exception.

"It's all right, mom," Becky said, smiling as she finished up and turned from the mirror. "Paul and I are just headed to a party just off the strip. I'm going to meet him there."

"I wish you wouldn't," her mom said, shaking her head.

"I know, I know," Becky said. "You don't like him."

"I'm not sure why you do," her mom said.

Becky laughed. Paul was a good guy who worked hard. And he was a very gentle soul. Becky liked that about him.

Becky kissed her mother lightly on the cheek as she went past and out into the hallway toward the front door. "You worry too much."

"Sometimes I wish you worried more," her mom said.

Then both of them laughed. That exchange had happened for every date Becky had ever gone on from a freshman in high school and all the way through four years at UNLV. It made them both feel better.

"Don't wait up," Becky said.

A minute later she was in her red two-door Toyota and headed out toward the Strip.

It was the last time anyone saw her. She just simply vanished.

And just like so many other missing persons, after no leads came up, her case went cold.

Thirty years cold.

CHAPTER ONE

April 10th, 2020
Las Vegas, Nevada

Retired Detective Bayard Lott ran a hand through his short white hair and sighed. They weren't supposed to find a body. Lott hated every time they did that. It was never the way they wanted to close missing person's cases. But more often than not, it was exactly how they closed them.

"Looks like we found Becky," Retired Detective Julia Rogers said.

Julia stood beside Lott staring down at the skeleton that was slowly emerging from the desert sand and dirt where it had been buried for almost thirty years, as far as they could tell.

Julia had on a light white blouse and a sports bra under it. She wore jeans and tennis shoes and a wide-brimmed white golf hat to keep the sun off her face.

Lott had on a short-sleeved dress shirt, jeans, tennis shoes and a wide-brimmed Panama hat. They had expected to spend time in the sun in the desert to the north of Las Vegas, so they were both also smeared with sunscreen that smelled like they belonged on a beach instead of out in the desert.

They might have looked silly and smelled funny, but he was in his mid-sixties and Julia in her late fifties and they were smart enough to take no chances. At their age, too much sun did not do well on either of them.

The open grave in front of them was being carefully worked by a couple of Las Vegas police's best forensic lab people. They were in white suits that had to be hot in the morning April sun in the desert. And they were being very careful to brush away sand and then shovel it into containers to be sifted.

Lott could visualize the wonderful college graduation picture of Becky Penn. She had been a beautiful woman with a promising future. She vanished on March 3rd, 1990, on her way to a party to meet her boyfriend.

It was her boyfriend, Paul Vaughan, that had reported to Becky's mother three hours after they were supposed to meet that Becky had not shown up. He had called concerned that Becky had been sick or something.

Her mother filed a missing person's report.

Nothing had ever come of it. The detective assigned to the case did some fine interviews, found nothing.

Two months ago, Retired Detective Andor Williams brought the thin file on Becky Penn's case to the weekly meeting of the Cold Poker Gang.

Lott loved the weekly sessions in his card room in his house. Retired detectives got together, played poker, and talked about cold cases. Then during the week between games, they worked the cold cases.

The Las Vegas Chief of Police had given the Cold Poker Gang special status to carry badges and guns because they had solved so many cold cases and wanted no credit for any of it.

For the retired detectives, it was just the sense of feeling valued that mattered and continuing at their own pace, without paperwork, the job they had loved for decades.

When Julia joined the group, she had retired from Reno because of a shattered bone in her leg where she had been shot. For almost two years, she was the only woman in the gang until six months ago two of Las Vegas's best women detectives had retired. Both had taken a month vacation and then joined the group.

Now the Cold Poker Gang often had seven or eight people at the table on a Tuesday night. There were eleven official members and every detective on the force liked helping them.

At any given moment, the gang might have eight or nine cold cases they were working in some fashion or another.

"Let's sit in the car for awhile," Julia said, turning from the grave.

Lott agreed to that idea. The sun was getting warmer by the minute and there was absolutely nothing they could do to help in that shallow hole. Getting Becky Penn's remains out of that hole would take time and painstaking work. Lott was just glad he wasn't doing the work, especially in one of those white suits they wore these days.

Lott got his white Cadillac SUV started and the air-conditioning running as Julia dug them both out a cold bottle of water from the ice chest sitting on the back seat.

Then they just sat in silence for a moment, cooling down and watching the two men in the shallow hole work.

Lott was always surprised at how wonderful cold water tasted after being out in the Nevada sun for a while.

"I can't believe we found her," Julia said after a moment.

"We're still not one hundred percent it is her," Lott said.

And they weren't, but that was just a technical issue now. They had figured out where she was buried exactly from notes in a journal left by her boyfriend, Paul Vaughan, when he killed himself twenty years ago.

From what they could tell when they got the journal, still stored with Paul's things by his sister, he and Becky had gotten into a fight and he had killed her.

The journal went on to give exact directions to where he had buried her and then what he had done to cover his crime.

Lott had found the writing creepy. Impassionate while being angry. Paul blamed Becky's death on her, taking no responsibility at all.

Lott had been upset that the guy was dead. But if he hadn't been dead, there was no telling if they ever would have solved Becky's cold case. They were lucky in a couple of ways. That he was dead and that his sister had just stored what few things he owned in boxes in her basement.

But something felt off to both Julia and Lott. And Lott couldn't put his finger on it at all. First, they had no idea why a killer like Paul would write down what he had done, then give exact directions to the grave.

And his sister had told them that Paul hated to write anything, let alone in a journal.

But it seemed, at least on the surface, that Paul had started the journal when he and Becky started dating and they had confirmed with Becky's mother some of the dates and times in the journal as best as she could remember.

So it all seemed real enough.

The second thing that seemed off was no one knew what had happened to Becky's red Toyota. The car had simply vanished and Paul made no mention of it in his strange journal. And he should have. Getting rid of that car had to be a lot harder than burying her in the desert.

Something was off on all of this, but darned if Lott could figure out what was bothering him about it all.

Then, in front of them, one of the two men in white suits working in the shallow grave stood up, turned and waved for Lott and Julia to come over.

Then both men climbed out of the shallow grave and one headed for their vehicle, pulling off his white suit as he went.

"Something went wrong," Julia said as both she and Lott climbed out of the car.

The other man who had waved them over had pulled off the top of his white suit as well and was working on a bottle of water. His face was covered in sweat.

"What did you find?" Lott asked.

The guy just pointed for them to look into the grave and kept drinking.

It took a moment for Lott to see it, but then he did.

Nowhere in any report did it say that Becky had three arms.

"There's another body with her," Julia said softly.

"Shit," Lott said. "Just shit."

CHAPTER TWO

April 12th, 2020
Las Vegas, Nevada

Lott set the bucket of Kentucky Fried Chicken on his kitchen table while Julia pulled out three bottles of water from the fridge. Andor had just parked outside in the driveway and was going to join them for lunch.

The smell of the chicken filled Lott's remodeled kitchen. In the remodel two years ago, he had put in the best counters, all new cabinets and flooring, and new appliances. But the floor plan of the kitchen was exactly as it had been when he and his wife had lived here.

His wife of thirty years had died of cancer almost five years before and it wasn't until Julia walked into his life that he could ever imagine enjoying the company of another woman. But now he did.

So now he and Julia and Andor, Lott's former partner back on the force before they both had retired to take care of sick wives, formed a team.

And outside of the nights with the Cold Poker Gang playing cards, the three of them often met over KFC in Lott's kitchen to talk over cases.

But Lott had a hunch today wasn't going to be much of a good lunch, no matter how wonderful the bucket of KFC smelled. The topic was Becky Penn's case.

Lott spread around three paper plates and Julia got some forks for pulling the hot chicken apart and some spoons for the sides that came with the bucket. They didn't often eat much of the sides. All three of them just loved the fresh chicken.

Lott came in the back door, his solid frame and balding head moving like a bull. He had a cold towel around his neck and was sweating.

Julia handed him a fresh towel to wipe off his face and head and neck, then she sat next to Lott at the table.

Andor dropped some files at the back of the table and all three of them dug into the chicken.

Finally, after pretty much demolishing his first piece and starting on a second, Lott couldn't take it any longer.

He looked at Andor. "Well, was one of them Becky Penn?"

When the other body was found in Becky's grave, the case had reverted back to the regular younger detectives. By the end of the day, the techs doing the digging had found a total of four bodies in that grave, all stacked on one another with a very thin layer of dirt between them.

From what Lott had heard, they were now doing ground radar sweeps around the grave to see if others were buried close by.

Paul Vaughan's journal had led them to the location, but he had said nothing about killing and burying other women.

Andor nodded, wiping chicken grease off his mouth with a paper towel. "It was Becky on top," Andor said. "Confirmed by remnants of what she was wearing, hair color, and the remains of her ID buried with her. They will run some DNA tests, but no one is doubting it is her."

"And the other three?" Julia asked.

"They don't have a clue," Andor said. "But they are treating all three as live murder cases at the moment."

"Three?" Lott asked.

Again Andor nodded. "They are closing Becky's case. Seems we solved another cold case."

Lott glanced at Julia who was shaking her head. He felt the same way. Becky's case was far, far from closed.

Andor just looked at them. "We're out of this one for now. You both know that, don't you?"

Lott knew they were. As long as the younger detectives considered the three other bodies open and live murder cases, there was nothing anyone retired in the Cold Poker Gang could do.

And actually, by doing anything, they might jeopardize the entire existence of the Cold Poker Gang.

They worked cold cases. Period.

That was the firm rule the Chief of Police had put on them.

Becky's case was officially closed and the other three were live murder cases.

The Cold Poker Gang was done with them.

Julia was nodding, and not looking happy.

Lott just sat there, not even interested in another piece of cold chicken.

"This day just sucks," Lott said.

"Yeah, it does," Andor said. "But we have to give the hotshot young detectives a crack at this first. Remember, we were young once as well."

"Speak for yourself," Julia said. "I'm still young, thank you very much."

Lott and Andor both laughed.

Julia smiled. "Not sure how I should take that laughing."

"Oh, oh," Andor said, winking at Lott.

"So what are the files?" Julia asked, indicating the folding files that Andor had at the top of the table.

"I brought them for storage here," he said, starting into another piece of chicken.

Lott laughed at that. He knew what they were without even asking. After the decades of the two of them working together, Lott knew how his partner thought.

Lott had Julia hand them to him and then without looking at their contents, he stood and put them in an empty cabinet above the fridge.

Storage.

"All four files for the bodies in the grave?" Julia asked, starting to catch on.

Andor nodded. "I'll get more from downtown and update them as the young hotshots find information."

Lott laughed and sat down and took another piece of chicken.

"And if they solve the cases?" Julia asked.

Lott laughed. "If they solve them like they think we solved Becky's murder, then we go to work on all four of the cases."

"And if they don't solve them, then we go to work on the cases," Andor said, smiling. "But that's going to be years down the road I'm afraid."

Lott nodded. "So the day officially sucks. We are officially fired from these cases."

"We move on," Julia said, nodding and taking another piece of chicken.

"We move on," Andor said, wiping chicken juice from his face again.

"There are no shortages of cold cases for us to solve," Julia said.

"Amen to that," Andor said.

Lott knew that was the truth. But he just hated failing, hated having a case taken from him, hated everything about this.

The Cold Poker Gang hadn't really solved a cold case. They had just found more murders that, more than likely, would turn into cold cases in a year or two.

Lott knew that all three of them hated failing. They didn't volunteer their time in their retirement to fail.

But sometimes it happened. Sometimes even the Cold Poker Gang failed.

Or, as they say in poker, you can't win every hand, even on good nights.

But down the road, way down the road, they just might get to play this hand again.

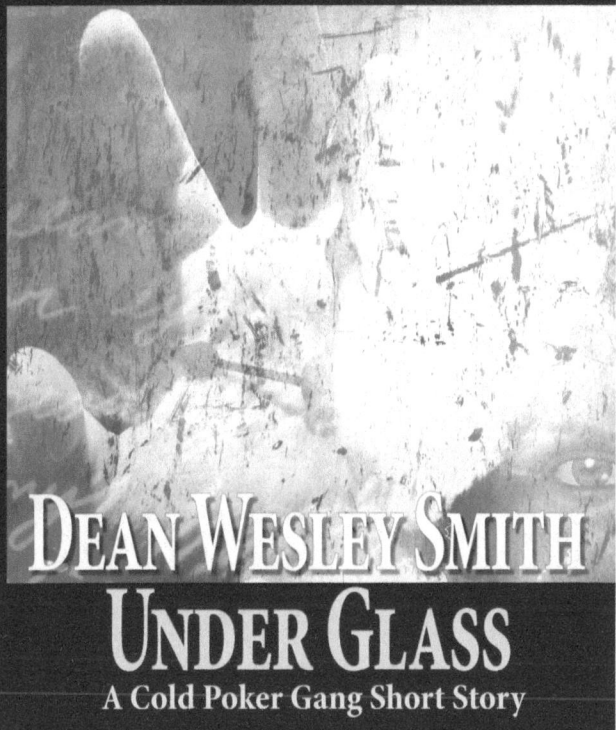

Smith's
STORIES

DEAN WESLEY SMITH
UNDER GLASS
A Cold Poker Gang Short Story

A woman's hand, perfectly encased in a box of glass. Found by kids in a field ten years before.

Retired Detectives on the Cold Poker Gang Task Force in Las Vegas finally get assigned the case.

What happened the decade before to the unknown woman?

A twisted Cold Poker Gang mystery short story.

CHAPTER ONE

Retired Detective Debra Pickett stood staring at the glass box with the woman's hand inside. One of the most famous and stupid cold case files there ever was in the history of Las Vegas. And that was going some.

Around her the sounds of the Las Vegas Police evidence storage area were muffled. The high rows of metal shelves stuffed with file boxes, all carefully marked, really cut down on the sound.

This area was the size of a large gym, only with very low ceilings. They were a good five floors underground here, and Pickett knew the storage went down for more floors and up for more floors. Lots of evidence that never got tossed for one reason or another.

The place had a bad musty odor that Sarge said he never noticed. Retired Detective Ben "Sarge" Carson stood beside her staring at the hand encased in glass.

So far neither of them had said anything.

It was one of those things that either caused jokes or silence.

The hand looked like it had been cut off just yesterday. Clearly the sealed glass box had kept it preserved completely.

It was a woman's hand, left hand, with a large diamond wedding ring on the correct finger. Whoever this hand had belonged to had been rich, or her husband had been. The diamond was very much real and valued back when this was found at over twenty thousand.

Sarge dug into the banker box they had taken the hand in glass out of and pulled out a thin file of reports about the hand. Pickett was sure it would be the same information that they already knew when Andor had assigned them this case.

They had the fingerprints from the hand by photo. And the prints hadn't been in the system. Tests without breaking the glass had proven the hand was real, as was the diamond. It had been found by kids in a field ten years before.

From what experts could tell, again without breaking the perfect glass box, was that the woman had been in her early thirties, was white, and had been regular size in weight, and more than likely had stood between five-six and five-eight.

No record of a woman losing her hand had been found and no missing person's case fit the description.

The case had gotten some laughs around the station, Pickett remembered that. Tough not to make hand jokes with something like this.

Then the case had gone cold.

Now ten long years cold.

She and Sarge and Retired Detective Robin Sprague, their third partner on the cold case task force, were now stuck with this hand, jokes and all. Pickett doubted they would make much headway with this one.

"I don't see here why they didn't crack this open?" Sarge asked.

Sarge had been in a different station when this came in, so he hadn't seen it the first time around like she and Robin had.

"The fine folks in the morgue decided that they would get no more evidence from it by breaking it open."

Pickett picked up the heavy cube with the hand in it and turned it slightly to show Sarge a tiny scar on the lower side of the glass.

"The techs used a tiny drill to get a sample of the air in the box and the DNA from the hand, all without disturbing anything or unsealing it. No need to crack it."

"The DNA was not in the system I assume?" Sarge asked.

"Nothing in the system back then," Pickett said, "but Robin is checking now and looking for familiar matches as well, something that

48

wasn't that common or easy to do when this was found. However, they did find traces of embalming fluid, so the hand, maybe the body before it was cut off, was embalmed."

Pickett, with the heavy glass box in her hands, studied it. The edges where the glass came together were seamless and smooth. Amazing the heat it took to do this kind of glass work didn't destroy the hand inside. This was a master who had created this.

"We need to track down who could do this level of work with glass," Pickett said.

"This sort of screams 'angry husband'," Sarge said.

Pickett had to agree with that.

So with one last look at the glass cube and the severed hand, they put it back in the box, put the box back among the hundreds of thousands of other boxes, and headed back to the clear Las Vegas air.

Pickett would be very thankful to get out of this room full of the evidence of so many crimes. It always gave her the creeps and this time had been no exception.

CHAPTER TWO

Pickett and Sarge sat in her Jeep Grand Cherokee and looked through the file even more. There had been a list of glass shops in the original file the detectives had visited. All of them checked out.

Pickett couldn't see a reason to try to go back to the ones still open at this point. That seemed like a dead end.

And besides, an expert said that the glass box, while impressive, could have been made by almost anyone with some basic skills of combining glass over flame.

So at this point, unless Robin came up with something on the DNA search, they were at a complete stop. So Pickett called her and put her on speaker phone.

Pickett and Robin had been partners and best friends when they were both active detectives. They still were partners, even though Sarge had joined the team.

"Find anything new?" Robin asked instead of saying hello.

"Nothing at all," Pickett said.

Sarge, who was sitting in the passenger seat just nodded.

"And no hand jokes?" Robin asked.

"I refrained," Sarge said.

"He did," Pickett said, laughing. "I was very proud of him."

Robin laughed, then said, "Well, I got a hit on the DNA. Looks like a close family member, like a sister. Had sent out for a kidney match five years ago."

"She still alive?" Pickett asked.

"She is," Robin said. "Name is Becky LaMont. She's a hairdresser but isn't working today. Sending the address to your phone. She has a condo near the University."

"Call you when we get done talking with her," Pickett said.

"Great work," Sarge said before Pickett hung up.

Fifteen minutes later they were parked facing a two-story condo complex that seemed to sprawl around a large park-like area. One of the older condo complexes that was for sure. It was ready for another coat of paint, actually.

They knocked and introduced themselves to Becky. She was a thin woman, very short, and more than likely a chain smoker, from the waves of smoke wafting from her apartment. She had big, beach-blonde hair and Pickett almost giggled at how Becky fit right into the stereotype of a low-class hairdresser.

No chance in hell Pickett wanted to be asked into that condo. She might have to burn her clothes afterwards because there was no doubt that smell would never come out.

"Did you happen to have a sister or relative who went missing about ten years ago?" Sarge asked, staying firmly planted right where he was outside the door.

Becky shook her head. "Nope, all my family is accounted for. I wish a few of them would go missing, if you catch my drift. Annoying ain't the word for them."

Pickett nodded. "Did you have a sister or close relative die about ten years ago?"

"Doris," Becky said, nodding and getting a very sad look on her face. "My younger sister. She was the best of us, married some rich guy, then up and died of cancer. Real sad. Tore me up something awful, let me tell you."

Pickett glanced at Sarge. Maybe, just maybe, they might have a lead on the woman's name who had once been attached to the hand.

"Could you give us your sister's name and also her husband's name?" Sarge asked.

Becky did, including where the husband worked, while also spending a few minutes telling them about all the good stuff her sister Doris had done and how much she had helped Becky when times got tough and Becky's second husband beat on her.

Sarge was the one that finally got them away from that door. Becky really was a natural hairdresser. She could keep a client engaged and talking on just about anything.

Pickett had her phone out and was calling Robin with the information before they reached the car.

"It's only eleven," Sarge said as Pickett started the car. "Shall we try his office?"

"Sounds like as good a plan as any."

The guy they were headed to see was Stan Knott, an attorney. Robin got back to them with even more information about Knott. He was well-respected, did a lot of charity work, and had never remarried after his wife and childhood sweetheart, Doris Knott, died of aggressive lung cancer.

His offices were comfortable, desert art and brown tones. When Pickett and Sarge showed the secretary their badges, they got right in to see Stan.

Stan had on a silk dress shirt, his tie off and collar open, and his silk jacket hanging on an antique coat tree in one corner.

The office had a huge desk, slightly cluttered, two chairs in front of the desk, and a couch and chair against one wall facing a large screen in the corner.

There was a framed picture of Stan and an attractive woman on the wall behind Stan with some of his degrees.

"Is that your wife Doris?" Pickett asked, pointing at the picture after they introduced themselves.

"It is," Stan said, pointing that they should take a seat. "So what can I help you with?"

"We think we found Doris's hand with a wedding ring on it," Sarge said. "Sealed in a glass cube."

"Is this some sort of joke?" Stan asked, his voice low and controlled, but clearly angry. "Because if it is, it is certainly not funny."

Pickett took a photo of the hand out of her purse. "This was found by kids playing in a field ten years ago now."

She slid the picture to Stan who stared at it and then slowly seemed to stop breathing.

He stood and moved over to the photo on the wall and took it down, bringing it to Pickett.

She looked at the photo. Doris's left hand was clearly visible and it sure looked like the same shape and the same ring.

"Did you bury your wife with her wedding ring?" Sarge asked.

"I did," Stan said, his voice soft.

Pickett took the photo back and gave him back his framed picture.

"This is how you remember your wife," Pickett said, pointing at the framed picture of the smiling couple. "We'll figure out what happened here."

Stan nodded.

"Do we have your permission to exhume your wife to double check and find evidence of what might have happened?"

Stan sat there for a moment, silent, then he said simply, "Of course."

Pickett couldn't even image what he was going through.

CHAPTER THREE

They had convinced Stan that he didn't need to be at the grave and didn't want to be. So besides the crew doing the work, Pickett and Sarge and Robin stood off to one side as they lifted the casket out of the ground.

The cemetery was one of the expensive ones in the valley, with real trees, mostly oak, and some palm trees along one side. The grass was freshly mowed and smelled wonderful in the warm fall day.

The morning sun was just starting to crest the distant mountains and the dew on the grass from the sprinklers was still holding on.

Once the casket was settled on a wooden platform beside the grave, the workers unlocked it and opened both halves.

"Shit," one of the workers said, stepping back and then turning away.

The other worker just stared for a moment before stepping back as well.

Pickett and Robin and Sarge moved across the grass so that they could see why seasoned cemetery workers had had a reaction like that.

It took a moment for Pickett to completely understand exactly what she was seeing.

There looked to be a woman's body in the casket, but the woman had no hands, no feet, and no head. Her dress had been torn open and both her breasts had been removed and her crotch had been cut out.

Pickett wanted to be sick. In all her years, she had never seen anything like this level of mutilation of a body.

Sarge turned to the workers. "Close this up and call the station. We'll fill in the active detective who is going to take this one over."

Pickett knew that was the end of this case for them.

With that, Sarge and Robin and Pickett turned away, heading back to their cars.

Pickett was glad for that. She sure didn't need to see any more.

And she really felt bad for Stan who still hadn't gotten over losing the love of his life. This was going to be very difficult to deal with.

"We did what we set out to do," Robin said as they got to their cars. "We solved the cold case of the hand in the box."

"And now we are off the case," Pickett said. "This just went active faster than anything I have seen before. And honestly, can't say I am unhappy with that."

"Neither am I," Robin said.

"I will agree to that completely," Sarge said. "I don't ever want to meet the sick-o who could do that to a woman's body."

"Or even try to imagine the reason," Robin said.

Suddenly Pickett had an idea. Someone had to have a reason and that kind of mutilation looked angry.

"Robin, before we go turning this over to the active side completely, could you look up a few things."

The morning so nice, the air so crisp, that Robin nodded and set up her laptop on the hood of Pickett's car.

"So what do you want?"

"Who was Becky, Doris's sister married to ten years ago?"

Sarge was looking at her with a puzzled look, so while Robin did a quick search, Pickett explained to Sarge and Robin her wild thought.

Becky had said that her husband at the time had been beating her and Doris stepped in and helped. That had to be a motive for some really deep hate.

"His name was Tom Davis," Robin said. "He's serving time right now in the state prison for two counts of double murder because he got angry and beat two women to death."

"Becky was lucky to get out alive," Sarge said.

"You're not kidding," Pickett said.

"Oh, my," Robin said, shaking her head. "Look where he worked during that time."

She turned the laptop around so that Pickett and Sarge could both see it. It seemed that good old violent Tom had worked at a glass-forming plant that made special windows and glass fixtures for hotels and casinos. He could have easily shaped that box with the hand in it.

"Seems we just gave the new active detective on this case a helping hand," Sarge said.

Pickett looked up at him sternly as he pretended to be innocent. "You were doing so well."

"He was," Robin said. "You got to hand it to him."

Pickett turned to her best friend who also pretended to just work on shutting down her laptop.

Then Pickett laughed and all three of them laughed.

After seeing what they had just seen and solving the case, a few jokes were required.

They were all headed for breakfast and they would be sorry they started this because she had a handful of her own.

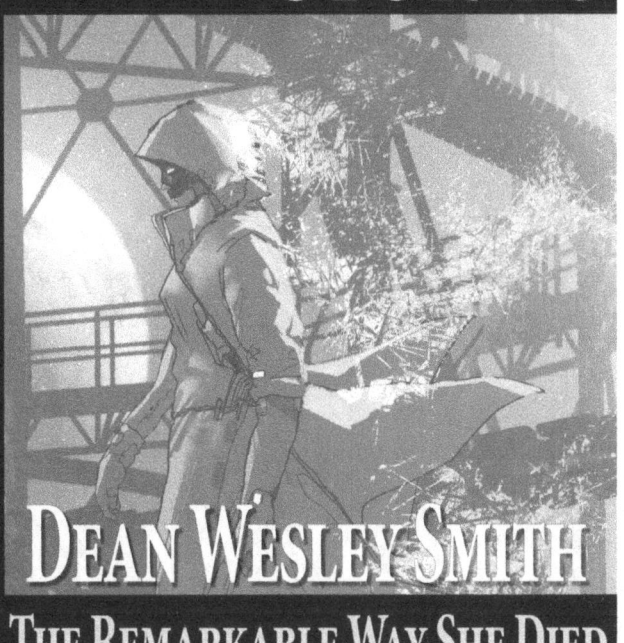

Smith's
STORIES

DEAN WESLEY SMITH
THE REMARKABLE WAY SHE DIED
A Cold Poker Gang Short Story

Picket and Sarge, two recently retired Las Vegas Detectives volunteer their time for the Cold Poker Gang task force that solves cold cases. Plus, they fell in love along the way.

Connie Dipkin's case remains at the top of the strange cold cases of all time in Las Vegas, and for Las Vegas, that says a lot.

She died standing up, in the middle of a sidewalk, with no wounds, nothing medical. And she stood there dead for three hours before someone noticed. A real cold case puzzle for Picket and Sarge.

THE REMARKABLE WAY SHE DIED

Retired Las Vegas Detective Debra Pickett had seen a lot of death over her decades-long career. And now that she was a member of the Cold Poker Gang task force with the mission to solve cold cases, she saw even more.

But how Connie Dipkin had died was maybe the strangest of them all.

She had died standing up, alone, in the middle of a sidewalk. She had no marks on her body, no wounds, nothing medical or poison that anyone could find.

And she had remained standing in the middle of that sidewalk, completely dead, for almost three hours before someone actually noticed something was wrong with her.

That alone shouldn't have been possible, but yet it had happened. There was even surveillance film of her from the moment she died, completely alone, until the police arrived three hours later.

One moment Connie was walking along seemingly just fine. Then she slowed and just stopped.

The day had been a nice, calm spring day in 2010, no winds, not too hot either.

The medical examiner had labeled Connie's death as unexplained, thus it was investigated. Since nothing was ever found to push it toward natural causes or murder, the case went cold.

And now Pickett was holding the thin summary file in her hand while sipping her morning coffee and waiting for Retired Detective Ben "Sarge" Carson to get out of the shower and get dressed.

Around her the morning Las Vegas sun filled their large condo with bright light. It was late October and the weather was about as perfect as it got here in the valley.

Their three cats, Pete, Ree, and Nose, had finished their morning routine of chasing each other through the place, followed by bathing, which was now followed by naps in the sun.

This morning Ree, a large orange tabby, had taken over one of the brown armchairs, while Nose, a black-and-white tuxedo occupied one end of the tan cloth couch and Pete, another large orange tabby, the other end.

Pickett loved those three cats and couldn't imagine this large place without them. They gave it life and energy.

At the moment it was nap energy, but still energy.

And massive cuteness.

Their condo had been decorated in shades of wood and tan and browns, sort of like the desert, only richer. And the kitchen she stood in was state-of-the-art modern, with white granite counters and a fridge that was larger than anything Pickett had seen before. Sarge had once said that a small family could live in the stupid thing. Pickett had not disagreed.

But what she loved more than anything else about their penthouse condo was the natural light that flooded the entire main room and kitchen. Even though they were on the top of one of downtown Las Vegas's largest buildings, it felt like the outside was being invited in, but without all the heat and wind.

Behind her Sarge came from the master bedroom area, his thick silver and gray hair still damp. He had on a light green dress shirt with rolled up sleeves and jeans. He had his badge on his belt and his gun in his holster under his arm.

She wore her normal as well, this time a tan silk blouse and jeans. She carried her gun and badge the same way Sarge did.

Every morning she was struck by how handsome he was with his deep hazel eyes and square jaw. She couldn't believe he had fallen in love with her and how lucky she was to find him this late in life.

They had only been together for a year now, but it felt like she had always known him.

And even though she was a lot shorter than he was at five-four, people said they made a great couple. More than likely it was because they were both always smiling and laughing and joking.

She handed him a cup of coffee and he took a sip, then glanced at the Connie Dipkin file.

"Any idea on that one?" he asked.

Pickett just shook her head. "Never seen a dead person remain standing before."

Sarge laughed. "That's a new one on me as well. Seen a couple vics propped up, one against a jukebox like in the song, but never standing on a sidewalk right out in the open."

"I was at one funeral," Pickett said, "where they stood the deceased near a pool table with a pool cue in his hand."

"Now that's weird," Sarge said.

"It actually felt sort of right for the guy who had died. Creepy, but right."

"To each his own," Sarge said, shaking his head.

"I'm not sure this was murder," Pickett said, pointing to the file on the counter.

Sarge took another sip of his coffee and nodded to that. "Let's hope Robin and her magic computers can come up with something, because I got nothin'."

"I'm still stuck on the woman dying standing up," Pickett said.

Retired Detective Robin Sprague was Pickett's best friend and when they had been active detectives, they had been partners. Now the three of them worked together on cold cases for the task force. Pickett and Sarge did the legwork while Robin did all the computer work.

Together they had solved a lot of cases in just a year working together. Sometimes Pickett and Sarge found the leads, other times Robin did with her computer. They had balanced well.

Sarge finished his coffee and they both put on light jackets to cover their badges and guns, then headed out for the five-block walk to breakfast at the Golden Nugget Buffet.

Pickett loved the morning walk and the routine of it. They ate at the Golden Nugget Buffet every morning and Pickett never got tired of the food because when she wanted, she just changed it up and ate something different. And she never had to do dishes. Or cook. Good food, someone to wait on her, no dishes to wash. To her, that was retirement heaven.

Robin was already there and eating, completely absorbed in reading something on her computer.

While Pickett was thin and short, Robin was solid and square, like a swimmer. She wasn't overweight in the slightest, just solid. She had always been that way.

Sarge and Pickett got their breakfast from the buffet and went back to sit with Robin. The three of them had the same table every morning, away from the tourists on the other side of the room near a massive wall of windows looking out over the hotel pool.

The room was decorated in oak tones, lots of plants, and brass everywhere. It actually worked as a décor and felt comfortable. And the staff knew the three of them and saved their table every morning and also made sure to not sit anyone close to them. Sarge had asked for that favor and made sure he tipped generously to keep the favor alive.

They talked about cats through most of breakfast until Robin smiled and said, "I know what killed Connie Dipkin."

Sarge laughed and Pickett just shook her head. That was so like Robin to do something like that.

"Connie was injected with a very rare drug out of Australia that causes slow paralysis of the muscles. The drug shut off her breathing and stopped her heart."

Robin got out a picture of Connie standing on the sidewalk, dead.

"Three reasons she stayed standing," Robin said. "One, there was no wind to knock her down and other people on the sidewalk never touched her. Two, the drug froze her muscles just long enough for rigor to start to set in as the drug cleared. Three, her large shopping bags served as balances."

Pickett stared at the picture. Connie was holding a shopping bag in each hand. And the two bags were wide and low, close to the sidewalk.

"I'll be go to hell," Sarge said. "Strangest thing I have ever seen."

"So how come no one spotted the poison in her system?" Pickett asked.

"Because by the time they found her it was gone," Robin said. "If she had fallen over and died, the tests would have spotted the poison. But since she died standing and remained standing until rigor started to take over, the poison was no longer detectable with surface tests."

"So we have no toxicology proof of this?" Sarge said.

"Oh, we do I'm sure," Robin said. "If a test is done looking only for the specific poison, residual amounts will still be there. They just didn't do that test."

"And it can still be done?"

"Without a problem," Robin said.

"Well, that's darned fast progress," Sarge said. "Great work there. I thought this would be a no-movement case."

"So did I," Pickett said.

Robin smiled. "I got more. Once I came up with the poison, I learned how long it takes to kill a person and freeze them up. Exactly ten minutes."

"So you backtracked Connie's movements?" Pickett asked, smiling.

Robin always had a way of being ahead of puzzles like this one, one of the many things Pickett loved about her.

Robin nodded. "Take a look at this. The detectives on the case originally had pulled all surveillance footage since from what she was carrying they knew exactly what stores she had been in."

Robin started an image of Connie just leaving a women's clothing store, her two bags balanced, one in each hand.

A man in his thirties, dark brown hair, glasses, bumped into her, excused himself, and went on into the store.

"Exactly ten minutes from the moment she stopped on the sidewalk," Robin said.

"And tell me you know who that man is?" Sarge asked a half second before Pickett could ask the same thing.

"His name is Preston Barker. It seems Connie's husband Jake had a secret. He was gay and meeting Preston on the side."

"And Connie had all the money, right?" Pickett asked.

"All of it," Robin said, nodding. "And Preston was working as a pharmacist, so he would know rare poisons like this one."

"Did the detectives at the time interview him?" Pickett asked.

"They didn't know he existed," Robin said. "Jake was deep, deep, deep in the closet. But Preston and Jake are now married and living happily on Connie's money."

"Not for much longer," Sarge said.

Pickett could only agree to that with a smile.

"We have enough evidence to actually get an arrest on this?" Pickett asked.

"The tests will find the traces of the drug that killed her and its time to take effect. I am sure there is evidence of him ordering the poison somewhere, and that film will cinch the deal," Robin said.

"Got a hunch good old Jake will roll on Preston, no pun intended, when faced with first-degree murder charges."

Pickett was certain he was right.

She looked at Robin, then at Sarge. "I think Robin should make the call on this one since she did all the work."

"Hey, I sat here and ate breakfast," Sarge said, smiling. "I should get credit for that at least."

Robin laughed. "Pickett, give him credit, would you?"

"Later tonight he'll get what's coming to him."

"Do I get extra credit?" Sarge asked, smiling.

"Only if you are a very, very good detective," Pickett said, laughing at the man she loved.

Robin waved her hand in the air. "More information than I needed."

Robin grabbed her phone to set up an appointment with one of the active detectives who could take this case and make sure all the details were in place for an arrest.

"In celebration of Robin solving this one," Pickett said to Sarge, "I'm going for dessert."

"Let me guess... bread pudding?" Sarge asked, smiling.

"Damn you are a good detective," Pickett said. "That might be even more extra credit tonight."

Pickett leaned over and kissed Sarge and he kissed her back.

"Would you two get a room," Robin said, shaking her head.

"No," Pickett said, standing and pulling Sarge to his feet. "But we will get some bread pudding."

"I'm going to need the energy," Sarge said.

All Robin did was groan and that made Pickett laugh all the way across the dining room.

Smith's
STORIES

DEAN WESLEY SMITH
USA Today Bestselling Writer

HALF A CLUE
A Cold Poker Gang Short Story

Picket and Sarge, two recently retired Las Vegas Detectives, volunteer their time for the Cold Poker Gang task force that solves cold cases. Plus, they fell in love along the way.

Vicki Dix's disappearance remains at the top of the strange cold cases of all time in Las Vegas, and for Las Vegas that says a lot.

Vicki, a well-liked attorney for a major firm, simply walked into her own home and vanished without a trace. Picket and Sarge decide to take one more look at the impossible case. Just one more.

PROLOGUE

October 21st, 2005

Vicki Dix spent the twenty-minute drive from her office near the university to her new home north of Las Vegas listening to a talk show about the new Supreme Court term. She had been a lawyer now for five years and loved everything about the law, including listening to political discussions about the high court.

And she didn't mind the perks that came with loving the law, like her new red Lexus she had just bought a week before. It had a fantastic climate-controlled interior and amazing sound system. In the morning, on the way to the office, she listened to a jazz station just to remind herself how good she had it.

In three days, she had a date with a guy she had met at a reception for a client a few days before. It would be her first date in a while, since her job had pretty much swallowed any free time.

And what little free time she did manage to get she had spent on her new home, getting it just the way she wanted it to be.

She clicked off the talk show as she pulled into the driveway of her three-bedroom ranch-style home and hit the garage door opener.

Her next-door neighbor, Sarah, was working on her yard and looked up and waved with a smile. Sarah had on a wide-brimmed hat that covered her skin. She was in her sixties and living alone, just as Vicki was, because Sarah's husband had died of cancer two years before.

Vicki chose to live alone. She liked it that way at the moment. And she loved her house and felt safe in it.

Sarah had encouraged Vicki to date and Vicki had done the same for Sarah, which had gotten a headshake and a laugh and a comment about being far too old to start over.

"Who said anything about starting over?" Vicki had said. "Just go for the sex."

Sarah had blushed and laughed and said she would think about that.

Vicki really liked Sarah. Vicki didn't really know anyone else in the neighborhood yet, but Sarah had promised to do introductions when there was time.

Vicki waited for the garage door to open and then pulled her Lexus inside as Sarah went back to working on her yard.

As the garage door rolled closed, it was the last time anyone saw Vicki Dix.

She vanished without a trace.

And her case went cold after one of the most massive investigations done by the Las Vegas Police Department.

CHAPTER ONE

October 19th, 2017

"There isn't even half a clue to start with in this file," Retired Detective Debra Pickett said, tossing the thin summery folder on the table in front of the remains of her morning buffet breakfast. "Not a damned thing has changed."

Around her the sounds of the Golden Nugget Buffet in downtown Las Vegas seemed a little louder than normal, more than likely because she was annoyed. Normally she never noticed the sounds of the tourists talking and laughing on the other side of the large dining room, or the clanking of dishes from the buffet area.

This morning the sounds seemed intrusive, like they were aimed only at her.

Retired Detective Ben "Sarge" Carson sat beside her just nodding. Pickett could tell he was just as annoyed. His square-jawed face looked more like a rock. He had a full head of silver-gray hair and even annoyed he was the most handsome man she had ever known.

She was much shorter than he was and four years younger at sixty-one. Her hair was still its golden natural brown and both of them kept thin by exercising and trying to eat healthy.

Pickett forced herself to take a deep breath and look around, working to calm herself some. The Golden Nugget Buffet was on the second floor of the main casino, isolated up an escalator and surrounded by oak planters and brass railings.

The ceiling was coffered with oak and brass and bright lights. On the other side of the buffet from where they sat, one wall was all windows and looked down over the huge hotel pool area and a shark tank. A tunnel slide sent kids through the shark tank and out the other side.

She and Sarge sat on the side of the large room away from the windows every morning.

The tables were oak, with brass chairs covered with brown cloth. Everything about the place felt comfortable. Pickett loved that she and Sarge walked here every morning for breakfast. That walk was one of the favorite parts of her day.

This morning had started out fine, with the air clear and crisp and the sky blue. The walk had been wonderful just like normal. They had eaten breakfast, then had looked at the new cold case file Andor from the Cold Poker Gang had given them.

The case was what had annoyed her.

Andor was a retired detective who was the liaison between the Cold Poker Gang task force of retired detectives working on cold cases and the Chief of Police.

Andor must have thought it funny to give them Vicki Dix's missing person's file. Pickett had been a full detective when this case hit. She and Robin, her partner, hadn't taken lead on the case. The Chief of Police at the time had done that, but the case had everyone working on it. Vicki Dix had been a young, up-and-coming attorney for one of the city's most powerful law firms. One of that firm's members didn't just go missing without it causing a lot of detectives to jump.

Pickett and Robin had been in the jumping detectives' bunch. They had found nothing.

No one had.

And that had made Pickett and Robin both angry at the time, the same anger Pickett was feeling now.

Vicki Dix had just pulled into her garage and vanished without a trace.

And now the brown summary file in front of Pickett almost exactly twelve years later haunted her again.

At that moment, Retired Detective Robin Sprague came off the top of the escalator and turned toward the buffet entrance. She didn't look that happy either. Robin had brown hair and was square, built like a swimmer.

Robin and Pickett had been partners and best friends for over twenty years when they were both active. Pickett knew all of her moods and Robin wasn't in a good one this morning, of that there was no doubt.

The three of them made a great team in solving cold cases. And so far they hadn't failed to solve one. Pickett and Sarge did the legwork, Robin did the computer side of things.

Looks like that record of solving them all was about to end with Vicki Dix.

Robin dropped her file in front of her seat, put her laptop bag on her chair, and without a word headed for the buffet to get food.

"I think this morning calls for dessert," Sarge said, pushing back his chair to follow Robin.

"Bread pudding," Pickett said, also standing. "I deserve bread pudding."

The Golden Nugget Buffet was known for its fantastic bread pudding, served all day long. Pickett normally tried to stay away from it because it was almost addictive. This morning was an exception.

"In my mind you always deserve bread pudding," Sarge said, smiling at her.

She laughed. "Deserve, maybe. Need, no."

"But we're getting some anyway, right?" Sarge asked.

She took his hand as they headed for the buffet. "You are damned right we are."

And now she felt better. The man she loved beside her, great food for breakfast, her best friend here, and bread pudding. It didn't get much better.

CHAPTER TWO

October 19th, 2017

Pickett finished up the last of the warm bread pudding and pushed the small bowl to one side.

Robin had asked about their cats, as she always did at breakfast and they had avoided talking about the missing Vicki Dix until Robin was done eating.

Then Robin got out a notebook and opened it up, which was the signal that the three of them needed to get to work on the case.

Sarge pulled his small notebook out of his shirt pocket and Pickett opened her notebook to a clean page.

"So let's start with what we know," Robin said.

"Not a lot," Sarge said.

"Her neighbor was the last to see her as Vicki pulled into her garage, right?" Robin asked.

Pickett nodded.

"There had to have been twenty detectives chasing down every possible lead," Robin said.

Pickett sat back and held up her hand. "Back then we eliminated every single person who worked in that law firm."

Pickett pushed one finger down on her hand.

"We interviewed every neighbor within a mile of the house," Robin said.

Pickett pushed down another finger.

"We looked into every detail of the poor guy who had an upcoming date with her," Pickett said, pushing down another finger.

"Forensic detectives looked over every inch of the yard and windows and doors," Robin said. "Nothing. No trace she left the house at all that night, since her home alarm was set from the inside and still on two days later."

Pickett pushed down a fourth finger.

"We backtracked over every restaurant she had eaten at in the two weeks before her disappearance," Robin said.

Pickett pushed down the final finger on that hand.

"My partner and I actually helped on sorting through any cases the firm had looking for any reason Vicki Dix had been targeted by an unhappy client," Sarge said. "Nothing at all."

Pickett could feel the same frustration she and everyone had felt all those years earlier. Vicki Dix vanished and no one knew how or why.

"So we know for sure she went into the house," Sarge said. "Or at least the garage."

"No, we know she went into the house," Robin said, opening up the summary file for the first time since they started talking, "because she turned on the alarm near the back door inside the kitchen area."

"And the alarm company was checked completely?" Sarge asked.

Both Robin and Pickett nodded.

"Every employee," Pickett said. "Robin and I were on that part of things back then."

"So she went into the house," Sarge said, "set the alarm, and there is no sign of any foul play or that she left at any point between that night and two days later when someone from work went to check on her."

"Two people went to check together," Robin said, looking at the file. "They were sent by one of the senior partners in the firm because Vicki not even calling in sick was unusual. They found nothing and two hours later the senior partner got the police to shut off the alarm and look for her."

"So when all other alternatives are proven impossible," Pickett said, "that means she never left the house."

Pickett then realized what she had said in frustration actually might be part of the answer to this.

"No sign of any blood or trauma in that house," Robin said. "Vicki had eaten dinner, had the television going, and poof she vanished."

"Aliens," Sarge said, shaking his head. "No other explanation."

Pickett punched him lightly on the arm. Anytime they ran into an impossible situation, Sarge jokingly said aliens had done it.

On this case, it seemed more logical than anything.

"Do you have a floor plan of the house?" Pickett asked.

Robin shrugged and pulled out her laptop and a moment later turned it so Sarge and Pickett could see the plan.

"Standard ranch with a two-car garage," Robin said. "Nothing at all special except a fantastic master suite with large bath and walk-in closet."

"Did she have it built?" Pickett asked, not sure where she was going with this, but clearly something had happened in that house to Vicki Dix.

"She did," Robin said a moment later after turning the laptop back around. "A year before she vanished. There are reports of interviews with the builders. They were all also cleared."

Pickett sat back. "Wish we could get into the place."

"We can," Robin said. "The bank took it back fourteen months after Vicki vanished, then the law firm bought it at auction a number of months later and haven't resold it yet. I am sure they will give us permission to go look around."

"Twelve years and they haven't resold it?" Pickett asked, feeling very surprised at that news. "Why not?"

"One of the partners said they owed Vicki that much," Robin said, in an interview four years after her vanishing, "to hold onto her home for a while to see if she would return."

"That firm can afford it out of petty cash," Sarge said, shaking his head. "I bet no one has even noticed it is still sitting on their books."

"Or they are waiting for a ten-year depreciation schedule to finish," Robin said.

Pickett bet that was the case.

"So shall we go take a look?" Pickett asked.

Robin and Sarge both shrugged and Robin took out her phone to call the law office to get keys.

"Why not go take a look? I got nothing," Sarge said, holding up and showing her the blank page on his notebook before stuffing it back in his shirt pocket.

She also hadn't written anything down.

This was impossible.

CHAPTER THREE

October 19th, 2017

Pickett was surprised at how well-kept Vicki Dix's home was as they pulled up. A frail-looking woman was working in one flower bed, a wide-brimmed hat shading her from the fall sun.

She turned and smiled at them as they climbed out of the car.

Pickett reached the older woman first and introduced herself, then Robin and Sarge.

"I'm Sarah," the woman said. "I live there."

She pointed at the house next door, also well-maintained.

"You been keeping up Vicki's home all these years?" Sarge said, smiling at the woman. "It looks wonderful."

"Well thank you, young man," Sarah said to Sarge, who blushed and smiled. "I don't have much else to do and Vicki vanishing like that bothers me every day."

"Bothers a lot of us," Pickett said. "That's why we are going to take another look around inside. See if something was missed."

Sarah laughed lightly. "As many detectives that there were crawling all over that place and the yard and neighborhood, not sure what you might find after all these years. But from what I understand nothing has been touched in there."

"Thank you," Pickett said.

"And thank you for keeping up this yard," Sarge said. "I'm sure wherever Vicki is, she would be grateful."

Sarah beamed as the three of them turned toward the house.

Pickett was always stunned at how Sarge always seemed to know the right thing to say at the right time.

It took a moment for Robin to get the front door open and then turn off the still-functioning alarm system. Another thing the law firm decided they needed to maintain to protect their investment, more than likely.

Pickett wasn't surprised that a woman living alone with Vicki's salary would have such an alarm. But the alarm made the case even more impossible, since it was never once turned off in those two days after she was last seen.

The power was still working fine and Robin turned on the lights in the living area.

"This is creepy," Sarge said.

Pickett couldn't agree more. A solid layer of gray dust covered everything and the house felt frozen in time.

And dead. Very dead.

It had been a very nice place in its time, of that there was no doubt. Comfortable furniture filled the living room area with a large television on one side of the room. The dining room table was close to the kitchen and if the drapes over the sliding door had been open, the view of the back yard and the mountains beyond would have been nice.

The sliding door still had the brace in the door blocking it from opening and every window in the house had the same braces.

Vicki's dinner dishes still sat in the sink, right where she had left them. Pickett remembered seeing a lot of photos of this place at one point. More than likely they were filed somewhere.

The garage was on the dining room side of the house. A hallway led off the living room to two small regular bedrooms and a small bath and then to a master bedroom with a large spa-like bath.

There was also a large walk-in closet still full of Vicki's clothes and shoes.

They tried to move slowly as to not stir up any dust. Their footprints were the only ones in the dust on the hardwood floors.

Pickett stared at all the clothes in the large closet, hanging on three walls. There was some open shelving under the hanging clothes and some drawers. In the center on the far wall from the door was a seating area. But something felt off and Pickett had no idea what.

"Robin, can you pull up the floor plan again for this place?"

Robin pulled out her laptop and put it carefully on top of a dresser, then a moment later had the floor plan.

The plan showed the massive closet. On the plan it was very large, almost the size of another bedroom. That would make sense if a young, professional woman was designing her own house for herself. If she liked clothes, she would design a large walk-in closet.

Pickett turned to Sarge. "Can you tell me how deep that closet is? Approximately."

Sarge shrugged and moved over to the closet and turned on the light. "Hard to tell with all the clothes and built-in shelves and such. I would say maybe twelve feet deep and the same wide."

"Oh, shit," Robin said at the same moment Pickett realized what she was seeing.

"That's what had bothered me," Pickett said as Sarge came back over to look at the plans. "That closet is square. It shouldn't be. The back half of the closet is blocked off."

"A safe room," Sarge said, shaking his head.

Pickett nodded. Vicki must have had it built privately after the regular contractor was finished. Often safe rooms were built by contractors from out of town and done without fanfare, so not even the neighbors would know about it.

Pickett could feel her stomach twisting. She so wanted to be wrong because she had always hoped that Vicki Dix was out there alive somewhere. But if Vicki was in that safe room, something had gone horribly wrong to trap her in there.

All three of them took out gloves and put them on. Then they carefully went hunting for the hidden switch that would open a safe room.

Sarge found it after ten minutes of dusty looking, hidden behind a moveable piece of trim on the closet door. As with any safe room, hiding the switch was the most important thing.

And the second most important thing was to make the walls impossible to break into.

Robin handed all three of them masks to put on, then when they were ready, Sarge hit the switch.

The seating area in the back wall of the closet slid away from them and then to the right with a loud raking sound. It was clear the false wall in the back of the closet was very thick, made out of steel plates, impossible to break into or break out of if something went wrong.

The lights in the room came up.

"Damn it, just damn it," Robin said.

Pickett felt the same way.

Curled up on the floor in the middle of the small room was the mummified remains of Vicki Dix. An open can of paint was off to one side with a paint tray and dried up brushes.

It looked, at first glance, as if she was painting her safe room.

"She passed out from the fumes in the small space," Sarge said, his voice low.

They all three turned and silently left the bedroom, taking off their masks as they headed for the kitchen and the front door beyond.

As they got outside Pickett peeled off her gloves and tucked them inside her mask to be thrown away.

The morning air felt wonderful. Not hot, not cool.

Just refreshing after being in that tomb.

Robin was on the phone to headquarters and Sarge said he would get them some bottles of water out of the car.

The neighbor Sarah came from around the side of the house and saw them all looking glum.

"Don't tell me you found her in there after all these years?" Sarah asked. "Oh, God, no."

"You might want to call it a day on the gardening," Pickett said. "This place will be swarming again with police in very short order. We'll come over and tell you what we found later, I promise."

Sarah started to open her mouth, then nodded and turned and headed home.

Clearly Sarah had hoped as well that Vicki Dix would just come home one day.

Everyone had.

But the problem was that Vicki Dix had never left home.

It had been her home, trying to improve her home, that had killed her.

That bothered Pickett more than she wanted to admit.

And right now Pickett wished they hadn't found Vicki Dix, that Vicki Dix would have just remained a legend among missing persons, with always a chance of coming home.

In a way, Vicki Dix had come home today. Just not in the way everyone, including Pickett, had hoped she would.

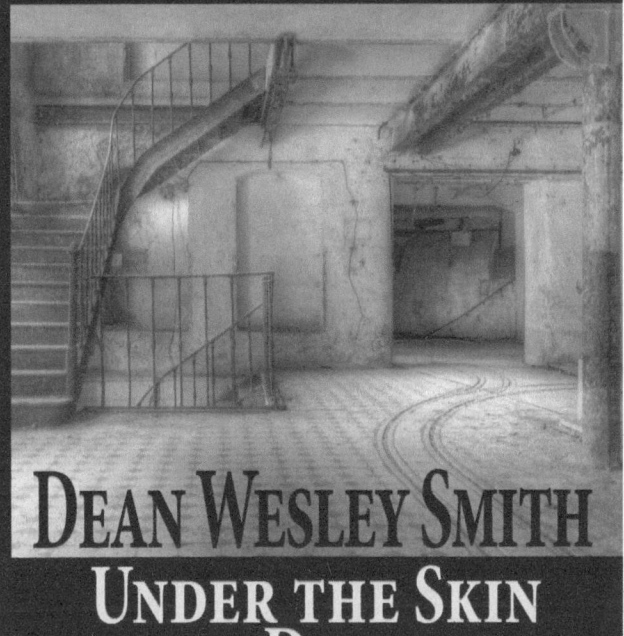

Smith's
STORIES

DEAN WESLEY SMITH
UNDER THE SKIN
OF DEATH
A Cold Poker Gang Short Story

Retired Detectives Pickett and Sarge and Robin working on a cold case given to them for the Cold Poker Gang cold case task force must figure out where a mummified body came from in the famous ruins of the Moulin Rouge Hotel and Casino.

The Moulin Rouge only stayed open for six months back in 1955, but the impact on race relations in Las Vegas and around the world lasted for decades.

Somehow they can't allow this case to stay cold and impact the history of the important and famous place.

CHAPTER ONE

The three cats were sleeping in the bright morning sun in the large living room of the condo. Retired Detective Debra Pickett just stared at them as she sipped her coffee in the kitchen, amazed that they didn't get too hot in the bright Las Vegas light.

Sarge's two orange cats, Pet and Ree flanked her cat, Nose, on the big brown cloth couch, all spaced evenly apart. She and Sarge had gotten the cats a year before as kittens, but now they were at full size. Nose, a black and white tuxedo cat was the girl and considerably smaller than the two orange male cats. But Nose seemed to run the house and the boys didn't seem to mind at all.

And all three of them were in top shape considering how much running they did through the two combined condos and up into the loft above the big condo. One thing both Pickett and Sarge had learned was don't get in the way of any of the cats when they were running. It was always a losing proposition.

"I see the morning napping in the sun has begun," Sarge said as he came down the hall. He always let her have the bathroom first and for that privilege she fed the cats and made the coffee.

Pickett kissed him and handed him his cup.

Retired Detective Ben "Sarge" Carson was the most handsome man

Pickett had ever seen. He had deep hazel eyes that didn't seem to miss a detail, thick silver-gray hair, and a square jaw that gave him a slight movie-star quality. And he was in top shape for a man in his sixties. In fact, he was in better shape than most men of any age.

She was much shorter than he was and four years younger at sixty-one. Her hair had not turned gray, but was still a rich brown for reasons beyond her imagining. She kept it short and easy to manage. Every other day they both worked out in the complex gym together and they walked as much as they could to stay in shape.

Today both of them were dressed in their normal way. They both wore jeans and tennis shoes. She had on a silk gray blouse with a running bra under it while he had on a blue dress shirt with the sleeves rolled up.

Both of them had their badges on their belt and their guns in a gun holster under their arms. When they went out they would both wear light jackets to cover the guns and badges.

Every day she was amazed they had been so lucky to get on the Cold Poker Gang task force. It was a group of over twenty retired detectives who met once a week to play poker. During the week they all worked on clearing cold cases. The task force had cleared so many cold cases that the Mayor had given them special status to carry their badges and guns.

And the really nice thing was that they could work on the cases at their own pace and never had to do paperwork. When they made headway on something, they brought in an active detective to take point. She loved that part more than anything else. They got to do all the fun work of solving the cases without all the crap of command and paperwork.

And the regular detectives loved the Cold Poker Gang because not a one of the Gang wanted credit for anything. When one of the Gang cleared a cold case, they just stepped into the background and let the active detectives take the credit.

However, at the weekly poker game, clearing a case always got a standing round of applause from the other retired detectives.

She and Sarge worked with Retired Detective Robin Sprague, Pickett's old partner when they were active. The three of them made a perfect team. Pickett and Sarge did the legwork, Robin did the computer work. They had closed a ton of cases over the last year or so they had all been together.

Today Pickett hoped they would get information that would close another. They had gotten the case file from Andor at the poker game a week ago. Andor was the retired detective who was the direct connection between the Gang and the Chief of Detectives. Andor picked the cases for all of them.

This time he had given the three of them the cold case of a body found two years ago after a fire in the remains of the old Moulin Rouge Hotel and Casino. The Moulin Rouge had only been open for six months in 1955, but during those six months it was the first integrated hotel and casino in the city. For six months it had the top entertainment stars of the time there, not only to perform, but as guests.

The casino had blazed a burning trail through the racial problems of Las Vegas in the 1950s. It hadn't solved them by a long ways, but it had at least forced open a few doors that led to progress.

It had to be one of the most famous casinos of all time, even though it had only been open for a very short time.

There had been dozens of attempts to remodel and reopen the place, especially after it was put on the historic register. But no luck for decades and a series of fires had pretty much left very little of the place remaining.

A body was uncovered during the last fire, clearly dead for a very long time and somehow hidden in the walls of the old hotel. The fire hadn't done the mummified corpse any favors, so all forensics pretty much managed to get was that it was a woman.

The woman's DNA was not in the system and there was just no telling how long she had been in that wall.

After two years the case of the body in the wall had gone cold, so Pickett and Sarge and Robin got it.

Last night Robin had called and said she had a lead and she would share it at breakfast. That was great. Anything was better than nothing. Pickett and Sarge had managed in one week to get nothing at all. They had even spent some time in the ruins of the old hotel, which the county owned as of last auction for the fifteen acres.

Both she and Sarge were figuring this case file might end up as unclosed on the small bar in the game room where they held the weekly poker game. There were only five files up there at the moment. That's how good all the teams of the Cold Poker Gang were.

So far, she and Sarge and Robin hadn't put an unclosed file on the bar. She hoped this one wouldn't be their first.

Staring at the three sleeping cats, they finished their coffee. Amazing how simply staring at sleeping cats can be entertaining, especially in the morning.

"Shall we go find out what Robin has for us?" Sarge asked as he rinsed out his mug and tucked it into the dishwasher.

Pickett handed him her mug. She wished she could say she was excited, but there was nothing about this case that excited her. It had just felt wrong from the start.

And she had a hunch Robin's information today wouldn't help that feeling in the slightest.

CHAPTER TWO

The walk from their condo in the Ogden Condominiums to the Golden Nugget Casino and Buffet was always wonderful. It was four blocks through the downtown area and then two blocks under the canopy of lights along Fremont Street. They did it every morning because eating in the buffet was a ton simpler and more enjoyable than cooking.

And the food was amazing. They could vary their diet depending on what they felt like since the buffet served just about everything for breakfast. For the last few weeks Pickett had had oatmeal, a slice of ham, a bowl of fruit, and orange juice. And today that still sounded perfect.

The buffet in the Golden Nugget was up an escalator from the casino floor and surrounded by oak planters and gold railings. As they rode the escalator, the sounds of the slots and people shouting at their winnings faded like they were climbing up into a peaceful cloud.

The buffet was huge and on one side had a wall of windows that overlooked the massive pool and shark tank that filled the center of the hotel complex. The ceilings were varied heights throughout the buffet with bright lights and oak trim. The tables were oak and the chairs a brass color with brown cloth.

She and Sarge and Robin liked sitting on the opposite side of the buffet, tucked away from all the tourists and windows. The staff knew them and saved them the same table every morning. And the staff, thanks to Sarge tipping them well, never sat anyone else close.

It was as if every day they had their own private dining area for their breakfast meetings.

Robin was already there and eating when they arrived and she smiled and waved as they came off the top of the escalator. Robin was square and solid, built like a swimmer. She had been Pickett's best friend for thirty years.

Robin's husband, Will, owned the city's top security agency. Robin was an expert on computers, but when she needed help, she could and often did go to Will's top experts. There was nothing they couldn't do or find it seemed.

It was odd that all three of them were rich, even though they were all retired detectives. Detectives seldom retired rich. Sarge had gotten his money when his parents had died and Pickett had gotten her money when her husband decided his secretary's large chest meant more to him than his money. Pickett had been very glad to take the money, actually.

That's how she and Sarge had both ended up with condos on the top floor of the Ogden, even before they met and fell in love. Knocking an archway between the two condos had given the cats a lot more room to run, that was for sure.

It was Sarge's turn to pay today, so Pickett headed straight for the food with a wave at a few of the staff. Ten minutes later she was sitting next to Robin.

"Will says hi," Robin said. "And how are the cats this morning?"

"Sleeping in the sun when we left them. As normal. Not a one of them even looked up when we said goodbye."

"The gods of the condos," Robin said, laughing.

Sarge set his plate down and shook his head. "Talking about the three cats who own us?"

"Who else?" Pickett asked.

They all ate for a short time before finally Sarge said, "So what is this information on this very cold case?"

"Two things," Robin said, finishing up a last bite of waffle. "First, it is pretty clear the body was stuffed in the back of a storage room and a fake block wall was built to hide it. I got that from looking at the old floor plan of the hotel and where the body was found after the fire and then looking at pictures. A small wall in the fire pictures wasn't on the original plans."

Pickett nodded. The Moulin Rouge Hotel had been made of mostly cinder block walls. That's why many of the walls were still standing in parts of the hotel complex even after over sixty years of desert sun and winter storms and numbers of fires.

She knew this not only because of all the times she had been to the site as a detective, but also because she had studied the history of those incredible six months the casino lived.

"Any idea when the body was put in there?" Sarge asked.

Robin nodded. "I think I know exactly. October 1st, 2001."

Pickett just stared at Robin.

Sarge had his mouth open, also staring at Robin.

"How in the hell can you know that?" Pickett asked.

Robin just grinned. "The body belongs to Cynthia Grimstad of Madison, Wisconsin. She went missing that day, reported by her husband, Ben Grimstad."

Now Pickett really was startled. And confused. "So you want to start over and explain how you got from a burnt mummified body to a name and date?"

"Yes, please," Sarge said.

"Computers are wonderful things," Robin said. "I set up a massive search through missing person's files from 1955 when the Moulin Rouge was open until five years ago. It would take at least five years for a body to mummify like this one was before it was burnt in the fire."

Pickett nodded.

"That's a few hundred thousand cases I bet?" Sarge said.

"A lot," Robin said, nodding. "But not impossible with all of it being entered into the police data base. Thankfully that task has been done for missing persons and murder cases now back to 1945."

Pickett could only nod to that. She didn't want to think about how many people went missing in Las Vegas every day. She had been told the amount once, but instantly forgot it. The number was just too high to consciously think about.

Robin went on. "I then cross-referenced any connection to the Moulin Rouge with every missing person's case."

"How many hundreds did that cut it down to?" Sarge asked.

"Only five cases, actually," Robin said. "One good thing about the place only being open for six months in its entire history."

"So how did you narrow it down to this Cynthia woman?" Pickett asked.

"The first four were easy," Robin said. "They were all men. The body found was of a woman. Cynthia was the only woman in the bunch with any connection to the hotel at all."

"And what was her connection to the Moulin Rouge?" Sarge asked.

"She and her husband were supposedly writing a book on the history of the hotel and had come to Las Vegas to visit it and explore and take photos. From what I gathered from reports, Ben's father worked at the Moulin Rouge for the short time it was open."

Pickett nodded. Family history like that, taking part in a major piece of history like that, would influence an entire family.

"So you know when she went missing?" Pickett asked.

Robin nodded. "She went missing just as the sun was setting on October 1st, 2001 when she and her husband supposedly got separated in the old ruins. Most of the big buildings were still standing at that point, so it was a maze in there."

"He reported her missing?" Pickett asked.

"Of course," Sarge said, shaking his head, the sarcasm in his voice not hidden.

"Within an hour after searching for her," Robin said, nodding. "Police did a quick search, but not much they could do since she was an adult and they figured she had just used the chance to get away from him."

"Were they having problems in their marriage?" Pickett asked.

"Detective on the missing person's case wrote that the husband said their marriage was perfect, but the detective contacted some friends back in Wisconsin who had another story about the two of them always fighting, especially about the book they were writing."

"Collaboration," Sarge said, "the quickest way to divorce."

"Or murder," Pickett said. She didn't like that assumption, but it seemed to hold true that the husband or wife were usually the main suspect. And often the murderer.

Sarge just shook his head. "So we solved the missing person's case and now have a sixteen-year-old murder case."

Robin nodded.

"Where is the husband?" Pickett asked.

"Dead," Robin said shaking her head. "He had moved to Vegas to keep looking for his wife and was killed in an automobile accident on the freeway seven months after she vanished."

"Vegas was not good to that couple," Sarge said, shaking his head.

Pickett could only agree to that.

Sadly.

CHAPTER THREE

They had closed a missing person's case from 2001 and figured out who the body was in the ruins after the fire. And Pickett felt as if she had done nothing. It had all been computer work. She and Sarge had flat made no progress at all and that was frustrating.

Sure, it was a modern world and computers helped a lot, but sometimes so did good old police work. Just not this time.

They had to step back from the case for a few weeks since it was now a murder case with a known identity of the victim, but Andor quickly had the Chief of Detectives give the case back to them to work.

So on a warm fall day, she and Sarge had decided that after breakfast they would walk over to the old ruins of the Moulin Rouge. It was just under the freeway and a ten-block walk from the downtown area. They expected to find nothing, but both of them felt restless enough to take the walk.

It had been years since she had even driven past the site. She had felt great sadness every time she had seen an article in the paper about another fire there.

The place was fenced off with signs warning of danger, but it was clear the fence was doing little to keep out anyone who wanted to go in. There were parts of the old two-story block hotel still standing and not much else besides weeds and the smell of old fire.

Where the main casino building had been was now just flat concrete with some cinder blocks stacked around.

All the windows and doors of the still-standing hotel wings had been boarded up, and gang tags covered many of the walls. The place had a heavy, sad feel to it as far as Pickett was concerned. Far too much history had happened here to ever have let this place end up like this.

She had put the old floor plan of the casino building on her phone and the location where the body was found in the back rooms of the old casino building. Both she and Sarge were fairly certain it had been the husband who had killed her, just because that was the most logical conclusion. No one else had motive to kill her and then go to all the work of putting her behind a block wall.

Robin was using her computer skills to check sales of blocks to the husband, but had come up completely empty. His actions had really been of a grieving man who had lost his wife in a strange city. The detective on the case had kept good notes of every visit the husband had made to ask about progress. The guy didn't seem to waver in the slightest as far as the detective on the case was concerned.

If he wasn't the murderer of his wife, Pickett felt really sorry for him.

The walls of the old casino building where the fire had burnt out had been torn down by the city right after the fire because of the risk of collapse, but it was still clear where everything had been if Pickett followed her phone carefully along the concrete slab.

The smell of fire, even though it had been two years, still choked the air and not even a slight fall breeze could clear it.

They found where the extra wall had been put up and some of the blocks, soot-damaged and broken for the most part.

The area where the wall had been built left not more than a two-foot space between the new wall and the old one. Clearly no one going into the old storage room would even notice, if anyone even went into this area of the building when it was still standing.

"I'm going to need a shower to get this smell off of me," Sarge said, standing in the warm sun and staring at where the woman's body had been hidden.

Pickett agreed to that. She was going to need one as well.

She looked around. The bright sunlight made the black of the fire remains even darker, if that was possible.

The place really did have a creepy feel to it, while at the same time a feeling of sadness from all the lost history.

"Let's assume the husband didn't do it," Pickett said. "We have a young couple from Wisconsin climbing around in here when this was still a building. They had expensive cameras and they looked clearly like tourists."

"A target for just about anyone," Sarge said, nodding. "Especially closer to sunset. Got a hunch this old casino was damn dark back then."

"So she's got a flashlight and a flash on her camera," Pickett said, moving away from the storage room outline. From the floor plan on her phone, this area had been for employees. A kitchen had been down a hallway to Pickett's right and a break room to the left.

Sarge came up and looked over her shoulder at the map.

Pickett was trying to put herself in the shoes of Cynthia that evening. Say someone did catch her in this hallway and killed her.

"Where would a person hide a body until a search by the husband and police was finished? It would take time to build that wall back there in the supply room."

"Good question," Sarge said. "There wouldn't have been many places in this old place in 2001 to hide her."

"And it would take someone who really knew the place, who had been studying it, to understand that a wall in that old storage room would never be noticed."

"True as well," Sarge said. "So Ben knew this place because of their research and any vagrant living in here would know it as well."

Picket looked back at where the wall had been built to hide the body. And she had a horrid thought.

She quickly dialed Robin.

When Robin answered, Pickett said, "Is it possible to figure out when Ben Grimstad flew into town and if it was at the same time as his wife?"

"Sure," Robin said. "Hang on. Easy search."

Sarge looked at Pickett with a puzzled frown.

Pickett smiled because that expression made him look even more handsome than he already was, if that was possible.

"Would you do me a favor?" Pickett said to Sarge. "Would you figure out how many blocks it would take to build that wall there where she was hidden?"

Sarge shrugged and said "Sure."

He turned to where the wall had been, stepping it off and measuring one of the broken blocks.

The sun was starting to get warm and standing in the burnt-out remains of an old building filled with history wasn't helping. She now wished she had worn her hat to at least keep the sun from her eyes.

Just as Sarge finished, Robin came back on the phone. "He came in three days ahead of Cynthia," she said.

"I think if you expand your search you will find him buying cinder blocks during those three days."

"Twenty-four of them plus mortar," Sarge said.

Pickett repeated that to Robin.

"I'll let you know what I find," Robin said and hung up.

"You think Ben came in and planned this, don't you?" Sarge asked.

"No place for anyone to actually hide a body in the old ruin here that the police wouldn't find unless that wall was already mostly built. He killed her, stuffed her behind the wall and finished the wall before calling the police."

"Makes sense, but something else tipped you off, didn't it?" Sarge asked.

"Camera," Pickett said. "Ben said he found her camera in the report that he gave to the police. If a transient or robber killed her, they would have taken the camera."

Sarge nodded. "Really good thinking and I am betting you are right. So how about I reward such wonderful thinking by scrubbing your back in a cool shower."

Pickett laughed. "That sounds absolutely wonderful."

She took Sarge by the hand and the two of them carefully picked their way out of the burnt-out ruins of one of the most famous casinos ever built.

Before they made it back to the Ogden and that wonderful promised shower, Robin called.

"You were right on the money," Robin said. "A guy matching Ben's description bought a bunch of cinder blocks and had them loaded into the trunk and back seat of a rental car two days before Cynthia disappeared."

"How in the world did you find that out?" Robin asked.

"The lumber yard out on the Boulder Highway got so tired of being robbed and bounced checks, they started automatically photographing every customer. They still have all the photos saved on the cloud now and when I gave them the day they pulled up his image and what he bought and a note about how strange it was."

"Damn I love computers," Pickett said.

Robin laughed. "That's usually my line. So how in the hell did you think to have me see if he came in ahead of his wife?"

"Good old-fashioned legwork that we will explain later," Pickett said, winking at Sarge as they got near the Ogden tower. "But in the next few minutes I'm going to be rewarded for my idea with having my back washed by a very handsome man."

"Way too much information," Robin said, laughing again. "Have fun."

"Oh, I intend to," Pickett said as she hung up.

All Sarge could do was shake his head and smile as they headed through the air-conditioned lobby of the Ogden for the elevators.

Pickett had no doubt it felt great to close this case. But the coming shower, after standing in those ruins of what had been a wonderful dream in its time, was going to feel a lot better.

At least now the history of the Moulin Rouge wouldn't be saddled with an unsolved murder. The history of that place needed to be focused on what it did for Las Vegas.

And whatever happens to those ruins going forward, Pickett hoped the memory of the six shining months the hotel existed would always be enshrined for many to study. And learn from.

Smith's
STORIES

DEAN WESLEY SMITH
USA Today Bestselling Writer

THAT HUMAN FEAR
A Cold Poker Gang Story

The Cold Poker Gang, a task force of retired Las Vegas detectives that meet once a week to play a little poker and work on solving cold cases given to them by the Chief of Police.

Retired Detectives Pickett and Sarge solved an eight-year-old cold case, but while doing so, they faced one of the most common human fears.

THAT HUMAN FEAR

October 26th, 2017

Retired Detective Debra Pickett stood in the shade of a tall rough-stone wall and watched a five-person forensics crew in white protective suits dig up a grave. Not exactly what she had hoped to do before breakfast this morning.

The Las Vegas sun was barely in the sky and already warm for such an early morning in October. Pickett was glad she had worn a light blouse and a wide-brimmed hat. She had brought a jacket thinking it would be cooler, but had left that in the car.

Beside her in the shade was her partner and lover, Retired Detective Ben "Sarge" Carson. He had on what looked like a cowboy hat to shade his eyes and protect his head. He wore a blue dress shirt with the sleeves rolled up and they both had on jeans and tennis shoes.

The grave the crew was working on belonged to a Mildred Case. Mildred had died eight years ago at the ripe old age of ninety-six, outliving three of her five children and her second husband. From what Pickett could tell, Mildred had had over sixty grandchildren and great-grandchildren and great-great-grandchildren at the time of her death.

The funeral had been very large, from what Pickett could tell from the records. But it wasn't Mildred they really wanted to dig up. It was what Pickett and Sarge thought was with Mildred. And it had taken days to get the court order to do this.

Days of nightmares and worry for Pickett.

She just hoped it would be worth it.

The entire thing had started when she and Sarge and Robin were handed a new cold case to work on. All three of them were a team and as retired detectives, had joined the Cold Poker Gang task force to solve cold cases.

Stephanie Donner, twenty-eight, and one of Mildred's granddaughters, had vanished on the same day as they buried her grandmother. The case had gone cold almost instantly.

So when Pickett and Sarge and Robin got the case, the first thing they started looking at was why the timing of the funeral and Stephanie going missing.

From what they could tell, Stephanie didn't even know her grandmother that well. She was an attractive young woman, standing only five-one with a bright smile and long, brown hair. She got top grades while in college and had worked up until the day she vanished as a project manager for a growing tech company.

She often said how much she loved her job.

She had a partner named Jill that she lived with and they had hoped to be married when the laws changed. Stephanie hadn't lived long enough to see that day, sadly.

Over the next few days after getting the case, Pickett and Sarge talked to dozens of co-workers and friends of the couple, without any success or leads. Everything they were told was the same as the original detectives on the case were told eight years before. No one had a motive to harm Stephanie.

The standard response they got was how nice Stephanie really was. That she had kind words for everyone she met.

Stephanie had told her partner that she was going to her grandmother's viewing at the mortuary, go out to lunch with a couple of cousins she hadn't seen in a while, and then go to the funeral before going back to work.

The cousins never saw her at the mortuary, although Stephanie did sign the visitation book, but about a half hour ahead of the people she was going to meet.

No one saw her from that point forward.

It was Sarge at breakfast at the Golden Nugget that suggested that they look into the staff of the funeral home past what the detectives had done eight years earlier.

Robin, Pickett's best friend and former partner when they were active detectives, had liked that idea and did her computer magic. Robin got the list of names from the funeral home and discovered that all but one had been interviewed earlier. The one guy named Angelo Clark had worked at cleaning and on the grounds of the mortuary. Angelo had vanished without a trace.

"Nothing suspicious about that," Pickett had said.

"The police had him as a person of interest as well," Robin said, reading from her screen, "but never found him before the case went cold."

So the only thing that was different in that funeral home that day was Mildred and her large casket. If for some reason something had happened to Stephanie in that short time and she had been put in the casket at her grandmother's feet, it would explain why Stephanie hadn't been found in eight years.

That's when Pickett started having nightmares.

Both Pickett and Sarge and Robin were sure they were right about this, even though they didn't want to be.

And what Pickett was the most afraid of was that they would find Stephanie with evidence that she had been alive when the casket was buried. That had Pickett waking up from nightmares two or three times a night the last three nights. Once she had been screaming so loud, the cats wouldn't even get near her for breakfast the next morning.

Sarge said the idea of being buried alive was his worst nightmare as well, but typical of Sarge, he didn't show that he was bothered by this. Sometimes the man was just steel.

But being buried alive terrified Pickett.

In front of them it looked like the team was getting closer to the casket and getting ready to hook onto it to lift it up out of the hole they had dug.

The court order was that if nothing was found, Mildred was to be just reburied at once.

The cemetery they were standing in was one of the most expensive in all of the valley. It actually had real grass combined with some desert plants and tall trees and palms that allowed a little shade. But with the angle of the sun this morning, only the stone wall along one side actually served as shade.

Every grave had a headstone, most ornately carved in some fashion or another. Mildred clearly had had some money to be buried here.

None of her family had decided to show up for digging up their grandmother. Pickett didn't blame them in the slightest. Always better to remember grandma alive than see her body after eight years in the ground.

Pickett had seen pictures of Mildred before she died. She had been a tiny, shrunken old woman with a bright light in her eyes and a slight smile on her face. Pickett had a hunch she would have liked Mildred.

Three minutes later the crew hooked the lift onto the casket and gently pulled it upward.

"Shall we get closer?" Sarge asked.

"No," Pickett said, shaking her head. "Robin had the right idea in staying home. I've seen enough dug-up bodies that I don't need to see this one."

Sarge nodded.

"Besides," Pickett said, "if Stephanie is in there, this gets sent to an active detective as a murder case. And if she isn't in there, we still have an unsolved cold case on our hands."

Sarge again nodded as the casket was set on a platform built to hold it. Then, wearing masks, two of the techs unlocked the large casket and opened both the top and the bottom at the same time.

Both of them instantly stepped back.

The man on the lift turned his head, while the other two techs also took a few paces back from the coffin.

Then the two who had opened the lid closed it at once and once again locked it.

"Looks like we found Stephanie," Sarge said.

"Looks that way," Pickett said as the lead tech started toward them, pulling off his mask.

"Detectives," the tech said. "You were right. We found a body of what looks to be a young woman wrapped around the older woman's feet in the casket. She was not embalmed, so we have to seal up the casket and get it to processing quickly."

"Thank you," Sarge said. "An active homicide detective will be taking over the case."

The tech nodded and turned to go back to his crew.

"Was she alive while in there?" Pickett asked before the tech got two steps. "Could you tell?"

She had to know. Otherwise she would keep having the nightmares.

The tech turned and shook his head. "No signs of any struggle. From the look of the dried blood and caved in skull, I would say she was dead when put in there. But that will be up to the morgue to make the call."

"Thank you," Pickett said, feeling relieved.

The tech nodded and turned away.

Sarge took Pickett's hand and they walked slowly back to Pickett's Grand Cherokee SUV.

They didn't need to talk.

They were done with the case.

They had given closure to the family of Stephanie after eight years of wondering and that was important. It was up to the homicide detectives to make a case against her killer and find him or her.

She and Sarge and Robin were retired. They only worked cold cases for the Cold Poker Gang task force.

And right now, today, Pickett was very glad that was all they did. They didn't have to notify the family, or open a fresh case with all the photos of that casket, or face the scum who had killed Stephanie and stuffed her in her grandmother's casket.

Pickett had done that job for long enough as an active detective.

And this case made her very glad she had retired.

She squeezed Sarge's hand as they reached the car and he smiled.

"Tough to let this one go?" he asked.

"Not in the slightest," she said. "Not in the slightest."

And with that, she drove them back into Las Vegas toward breakfast at the Golden Nugget buffet.

Their routine was to eat breakfast at the Golden Nugget Buffet.

She needed the routine right now.

She needed to feel alive and in control.

And maybe by next week she might be ready for another cold case.

Maybe.

Smith's
STORIES

DEAN WESLEY SMITH
USA *Today* Bestselling Writer

THE MISSING
A Cold Poker Gang Story

The Cold Poker Gang Mysteries feature a group of retired detectives who solve cold cases in Las Vegas. The stories always combine Vegas history with some compelling and suspenseful (and often creepy) idea.

This story gives a nod to D. B. Cooper Day, with a mystery about missing persons...who are just begging to be found.

CHAPTER ONE

It was D. B. Cooper Day. November 24th. Retired Detective Debra Pickett found that almost funny, in an ironic sort of way.

In front of her, on the white-marble kitchen counter, two gold detective badges sat, looking very out of place. For the past two years and seven months, they had been on a shelf near the kitchen along with some mystery novels and a few goofy awards she and Sarge had gotten when still on the force. Over two-and-a-half years those badges had rested there, out of the way, out of sight, and seldom talked about.

Now, of all days, on D. B. Cooper Day, she had brought the badges off the shelf and put them where Sarge would see them when he came down for his morning coffee.

When she and Detective Ben "Sarge" Carson had retired from the force, they had both joined the Cold Poker Gang Task Force, solving cold cases. That was when they had met and fallen in love, which neither of them had ever expected to do again.

The Cold Poker Gang Task Force had shut down in March of 2020 in the pandemic and now it was late November of 2022. Wow, that was a long time.

They had spent the time together, staying safe, waiting for their vaccinations to finally come around. And besides even exercising more than they had before the shutdown, one of the things they had gotten into over the last two years was celebrating strange holidays.

It seemed that just about every day was a holiday of something or another, and it had become not only a habit, but a lot of fun to try to figure out how to celebrate each holiday.

Now, the day the cold case task force comes back into active duty is the day to celebrate the most famous of all cold cases. A man using the name D. B. Cooper hijacked an airliner, let all the passengers off in exchange for a large bag of money, then somewhere over the Washington/Oregon border, parachuted from the plane and vanished completely.

Maybe Andor, the retired detective who ran the task force, had planned giving them this case today. She doubted it. Just not his style.

She picked up her gold badge and held it, feeling the once-familiar weight in her hand as she shifted it from hand to hand, then put it back on the wide stone counter of the kitchen. She had honestly doubted those badges would ever be moved again except to dust the shelf.

For so many decades that detective's badge had been her main focus in life, and for a couple years after she retired, the badge had been a symbol of her value with the Cold Poker Gang Task Force.

That badge and the cold case task force had introduced her to Sarge, the man she now could not imagine living without.

She was now sixty-three and her new husband, Sage was sixty-seven. But both of them were still in top shape and had managed to stay that way, even through the entire pandemic. They had actually gotten married this last summer, even though both of them had originally sworn to never do that again after their first marriages.

While Sarge was still sleeping, Pickett had gotten a call from her old partner while on active duty, Robin Sprague, who had told her the Cold Poker Gang Task Force was firing back up and she had a new case for the three of them from Andor.

"Same rules and restrictions?" Pickett had asked.

"Nothing changed," Robin said.

"Except the entire world," Pickett said.

Robin made no comment to that.

Pickett pulled up a barstool and sat staring at the badges for a moment, sipping on her coffee.

Around her, the morning Las Vegas sun filled their massive dual penthouse condo in The Ogden with bright morning light through the two-story floor-to-ceiling windows. At the moment, their three cats were nowhere to be seen. Pickett knew they were in the other half, spread out in the sun over two couches and an ottoman.

For the last two-plus years, she and Sarge had lived very comfortably here, first off ordering in all their food and supplies, then after they both had their first two shots, heading back out to restaurants that were open and struggling, not only to get out, but to try to help the struggling businesses.

And every day they played with whatever holiday it was that day, sometimes learning more about the holiday, sometimes just toasting to it in the evening.

But the daily holiday had become an important ritual over the last few years. And they both thought it weird and funny.

But it was also fun.

Now, below the massive windows, the city seemed to be back and growing. Las Vegas had life again and she and Sarge had spent a lot of time seeing shows and finding new restaurants and just enjoying living.

Part of Pickett didn't want to put that badge back on. But part of her did. She wanted to wait and see what Sarge thought before she decided, before she let Robin send her the new case. Pickett didn't want to be tempted by a cold case that was interesting. They had all been interesting over the years.

She just sat at the counter, thinking as she stared out over the beautiful city and the Strip beyond until Sarge came down the stairs. His full head of white hair almost glowed from the shower. He was, far and away, the most handsome man she had ever known, and what he saw in her, she'll never know.

He had on his normal jeans, running shoes, and dress shirt tucked in, moving easily, not at all like many his age.

He got a mug from the cabinet, poured himself a cup of coffee, picked up his badge and put it on his belt, and then sat down and smiled at her.

"We're back, I'm guessing."

She just laughed. She should have known there would be no doubt with Sarge. He was like her. He had lived for that badge and what it meant for decades. If he could put it back on, he would.

She reached over and took her badge and hooked it to her belt where she had normally carried it. Damn that felt great. Beyond great. She wasn't sure why she had even hesitated.

"We're back," she said, smiling as they toasted with their coffee mugs.

"What's the case?" Sarge asked, sipping his coffee.

"Damned if I know," Pickett said. "How about we meet Robin for breakfast like we used to do and have her bring the file?"

"Golden Nugget buffet never reopened," Sarge said.

Pickett nodded. That had been their meeting place for their first three years with the task force. She kind of missed it.

"Main Street Station buffet is open for breakfast," she said.

"Perfect," Sarge said, taking a long sip of his coffee and then placing the mug in the sink. "We can walk it like we used to do to the Nugget. You call Robin, I'll get our guns out of the safe."

"Are we really sure we want to do this again?" Pickett asked.

"I can't imagine not doing it until they shut us down again," Sarge said. "And besides, it's D. B. Cooper Day. What a better day to solve a cold case."

Pickett smiled, feeling the excitement flow through her for the first time in years. "I can't imagine anything else, either."

And she couldn't. They had made it through the years of pandemic, now it was time to go back to work.

CHAPTER TWO

The Main Street Station Casino was located near where the old Las Vegas train station used to be, and was decorated like a 1900s ornate station, with towering polished wood columns and massive beams thirty feet overhead. The front desk area even had polished wooden train benches and the front desk looked more like a front hotel desk from 1910 than anything modern.

The casino had an old-time feel to it overall, and they even scattered old and sometimes expensive antique furniture around. Massive plants dangled from the ceiling and the beams and this was the only major casino in Vegas that actually had windows all around. Most of them were stained glass, but they were windows letting natural light flood over the slot machines.

Pickett always felt comfortable in the place and this morning was no different. The walk was exactly five blocks and the morning wasn't cool enough yet to require jackets. Perfect Vegas fall weather.

Robin sat at a back wooden table under one of the massive windows when they got there, already eating. She looked almost identical to when she and Pickett had been partners. While Pickett kept herself thin and looking like a runner, Robin was always square-shaped and kept her brown hair short.

Robin and her husband ran one of the top security companies in the city, protecting everyone from politicians to major celebs.

Robin waved at them as they paid and then filled their plates before heading to the table to join her. Pickett got her normal eggs and bacon and oatmeal while Sarge did what he always did in a buffet and filled his plate with a half-dozen different forms of meat. Even for breakfast.

"Happy D. B. Cooper Day," Sarge said to Robin as he sat down across from her.

"Happy day to you as well," Robin said, smiling. "And Andor is really playing with us."

Pickett looked at her partner. She knew that grin on Robin's face. It meant this case had something really strange about it.

"How is that?" Pickett asked as she sat down next to Sarge.

Pickett slid a brown file toward her across the table that had stamped on it, "Copy."

Pickett glanced at the name on the file.

Becky Williams.

"No chance!" Pickett said.

Sarge glanced up from his plate and Pickett turned the folder so he could see the name on it.

Sarge just shook his head. "Andor is in a mood to restart us, I see."

Pickett just nodded and started into her eggs.

Becky Williams went missing on November 24th, 1971, the exact same day D. B. Cooper vanished up in Oregon and Washington.

But even though that was before Pickett's time on the force, everyone knew this case by heart. Becky Williams had been a twenty-one-year-old college kid, liked by everyone, working in a local restaurant while going to school.

Rich parents, a million friends, no reason at all to vanish.

She had lived in the Independence Apartments, which were high-end apartments, recently remodeled at the time. Her parents paid for the place and she even had a car.

The Independence was a historical building in Las Vegas, built back in the Prohibition days and was said to have had a speakeasy in its basement at one point.

When Becky lived there it had been completely remodeled, keepings its old art deco look while making the apartments modern for 1971, and the basement where the speakeasy was rumored to be was a laundry room for the tenants.

Becky had gone into the building, into her apartment on the second floor, and completely vanished. The building had security, a doorman, and cameras and there was no evidence at all she ever left the building. At least not by normal means.

But no crime scene was ever found and every inch of the building was searched. She or her body never turned up anywhere.

The D. B. Cooper of Las Vegas.

The belief was that somehow she never left the building and now haunted it.

Andor had given them Las Vegas's most famous cold case to bring them back after two years. Pickett had no idea why, other than he somehow knew they were going to celebrate D. B. Cooper Day today.

What the hell, maybe they could solve them both at the same time.

CHAPTER THREE

Turned out that after they finished eating and started talking about the case, a reason for Andor's madness came clear.

And why today.

It seems the Independence was being remodeled once again into high-end condos this time. It had sat empty and boarded up for almost a decade, but the historical designation for the building hadn't let anyone tear it down.

So now, spending more millions than it would have cost to build it new, they were going to remodel. And today they were tearing out the interior, including Becky's old apartment. So Andor wanted them to be there, see if Becky's body turned up somehow.

To Pickett, that made a lot of sense, so after finishing eating, she and Sarge walked home, put on old tennis shoes, older clothes that wouldn't matter if they got ruined or dirty, and then walked the four blocks to the Independence.

It was surrounded by a high construction fence and had a bunch of equipment hauling out debris from the inside through what used to have been a massive front door.

Robin was just parking down the street and the foreman handed all three of them helmets and then pointed to a guy who clearly didn't look like a construction worker.

"Architect," the foreman said. "He'll show you around."

They introduced themselves to Baker Dunn, who seemed instantly passionate about this ancient old building.

Baker was a young architect as far as Pickett could tell, with slightly longer brown hair and clear skin that made him look younger than she guessed he was.

He had green eyes and they just lit up with the passion of the project in front of him.

"You're going to have to be careful, Detectives," he said. "Some of the old walls and flooring have deteriorated pretty badly. We're tearing it all out as fast as we can, saving what we can."

Pickett admired Baker's passion and his ability to see what was possible from a mold-smelling pile of wood as far as she was concerned. She liked that most buildings in Vegas, when they reached the last of their useful life, were just torn down. Kept the city fresh and modern-looking.

"Are you familiar with the Becky Williams missing person case?" Robin asked Baker.

He laughed. "Anyone around this building for any amount of time knows every detail."

"So can you show us what's left of Becky Williams' old apartment?" Sarge asked.

"I can," Baker said, nodding. "But we got most of the wallboard off and the floors torn up in there. Just no place for a body to have stayed hidden since 1971."

With that he turned and led them through the big archway, around a pile of mold-smelling pieces of wood and flooring, and up a staircase to the right. To Pickett the staircase had almost an old southern mansion feel to it, sweeping up and curving to the left over the large main foyer. Beautiful, yet at the same time creepy in its ruined state of peeling paint, remnants of carpet, and broken railings.

The hallway on the second floor was lit by a few construction lamps and it led to the left. It was narrow like hallways of the time and Baker led them single-file to the second door on the right.

"Stay on the plywood covering the joists," he said as he stepped aside and let them into the apartment.

As Baker had told them, most of the walls were gone, leaving only old studs that they could see through into the apartments on either side.

It didn't take long to see that there was nothing to hide a body. Even the ceiling above was gone, showing the temporary plywood on the floor of the apartment above.

Where a kitchen and bathroom had been only capped off pipes remained.

Sarge nodded, then turned to Baker who was standing in the door. "Can you show us where the old speakeasy was supposed to have been?"

"Sure," he said and started back toward the stairs, leaving them to follow.

Pickett understood why Sarge had asked that question. The best guess over the last fifty-one years was that somehow she had found her way into the walled off speakeasy and then gotten trapped and died. But in all the years, no one had found where that speakeasy might have been. All the space for it was supposedly used by a furnace room and the laundry room when it was remodeled before Becky moved in.

But with no evidence at all that Becky left the building on the day she disappeared, and her apartment and every apartment being completely searched more than once, only the old speakeasy was left to answer this mystery.

Pickett didn't give it much hope.

CHAPTER FOUR

Baker led them back down the grand staircase, then around and down another regular flight of stairs under the larger staircase. Again, it was lit by construction lamps and the smell of mold and mildew got a lot worse. Pickett had no doubt she would be throwing these clothes away when she got home.

At the bottom was a large room that clearly had been plumbed for washing machines that were long gone. A shelf was built into one wall and was half torn out.

"This was supposedly the main part of the speakeasy," Baker said. Then he moved over to a door and shoved it open, stirring up even more mold and mildew smell if that was possible.

He clicked on a light just inside the door, showing a couple more construction lamps and the remains of a couple large furnaces.

"Here was the back room and supposedly storage for the speakeasy."

Pickett looked around, trying to get herself to imagine this as a hidden speakeasy. The floor was concrete, but the ceiling above was just regular wooden joists.

"Anyone would hear the music from this place through that floor," Pickett said. "It would have never stayed hidden."

She pointed up and Sarge nodded.

So did Robin.

"Speakeasies had to be sound-proof completely," Robin said.

Baker just sort of looked puzzled which gave his young face an innocent look.

"My bet is that the speakeasy was below this concrete floor," Sarge said. "But how come no one in fifty years has found a way down into it?"

"Pretty certain there is nothing down there," Baker said.

"Not thinking like a criminal," Pickett said to Baker, smiling.

Sarge laughed. "I knew there was a reason I married you."

"You married me? I remember I married you."

"Kids," Robin said, shaking her head. Then she turned to Baker. "You run ground-penetrating radar on this floor?"

He shook his head. "Saw no reason to."

"So," Sarge said to Baker, "Could you get some of your crew down here to pull down some walls and see if we can find a staircase down."

He nodded and headed back up the stairs while the three of them slowly explored, looking for something that residents of this building and detectives had missed for fifty years.

Yeah, fat chance of that.

Baker brought the three of them face coverings, commercial grade for the dust that was about to be stirred up.

Then two of his men sat up three heavy-duty fans to blow as much of the dust that was going to be generated back up the stairs.

And two other men brought down a large flexible pipe large enough for a person to crawl through and sat that up pumping in fresh air. When everything was started it felt like a windy day in the basement.

Pickett thought that very strange, but was very glad they did it.

"Any idea where you would like to start, Detectives?" Baker asked once everything and everyone was ready to go.

Sarge pointed to the built-in shelf and stepped back with Pickett and Robin to the other side of the room.

The crew made quick work of the shelf, kicking up as little dust as possible as two other workmen carried the wood up the stairs and out. Pickett stood beside Sarge and Robin and just watched. She had a feeling about this. Not a good feeling.

Behind the shelf was a wall that looked original to the building and Baker indicated that his men should tear it out as well.

Once the dust cleared enough to see what was behind the wall, and in the wall, Pickett knew they were on the right track.

Baker had his men stand back and he moved over and shown his flashlight between the old studs of the wall on what looked to be frayed rope and a giant counterweight sitting on the base of the wall. Pickett guessed that weight weighed as much as she did, if not more.

Pickett looked at it and said, "I think we just figured out what happened to Becky Williams."

Sarge nodded. "The rope broke."

CHAPTER FIVE

The rope seemed to vanish over the top of the wall. Pickett knew, just as they all did, that the counterweight had been used to open and close a very heavy door into a soundproof speakeasy below them.

But where was that entrance? And why hadn't anyone seen it in all the searches of this basement?

Baker gave his men a break and the four of them stood staring at the large counterweight in the wall.

Pickett looked over at the open stairs leading upward and then at the ceiling above them. Neither of them would block that much sound.

"So if sound was critical," Pickett said, "the door can't be in this room."

"Is that door original to the house?" Sarge asked Baker, pointing to the door leading into the back storage area.

"It is," Baker said. "The remodeling in the late 1960s didn't move it."

"So with that door closed," Pickett said, "it would offer some sound protection when the door to the speakeasy was opened."

"It would," Baker said and all four of them moved into the next room over.

The floor there was also old concrete and the walls also looked to be concrete. There was a door on the other side of one of the old furnaces.

"That go up a back staircase?" Sarge asked, pointing at the door, and Baker confirmed that it did.

"So either the speakeasy entrance or a service entrance or both," Robin said.

Pickett and Sarge both turned around to face the open door to the old laundry room.

"That rope vanishes up into that area," Sarge said, pointing to an area behind the open door.

Pickett moved over and closed the heavy door with a thud. It clearly had not been closed in decades and she had to really push it over the floor to get it closed.

And the moment she did, that room got even more frightening. Before it just smelled, now it felt dangerous.

"The large counterweight was used to help lift something," Sarge said. "So look for a door near here in the floor."

Pickett was about to give up as all four of them spent the next ten minutes studying everything on that floor until Sarge said, "Here."

He was pointing to an area behind the door they had closed.

It took Pickett a minute to see it, but the door wasn't really a door, it was a half-door in the wall and a half-door in the floor. Kind of like a regular door had been bent in half.

Pickett had no idea how that would work, but once they brushed the dust out of the cracks in the floor and on the wall, it seemed strange enough to be possible.

Baker suddenly got excited. "Only seen pictures of these out of Europe," he said. "The wall portion slides back and up into the wall."

He showed the motion with his hand in the direction it would go up.

"This lower part should slide down and sideways under the floor, revealing a staircase down right here."

He looked around. "There should be a way to move those slabs from this side without destroying them, even without that counterweight that would move that top slab up."

"Imagine a raid on this place," Pickett said. "It couldn't be anything a cop might trigger accidently."

"And it would have to be close and accessible when the door was closed. This would never work with that door open."

Sarge immediately went to the back door trim and carefully ran his fingers along it until he said, "Got it."

He tried to pull what seemed to be a lever down, but couldn't move it.

"Need a small crowbar or hammer and more than likely a few of your men."

Baker nodded, opened the door back up to the staircase and the other room, much to Pickett's relief and got the tool and three men.

When they were all back inside, he again closed the door and handed Sarge a claw hammer.

Sarge got the hammer behind the metal lever and pulled it down and with a grinding sound the small section of the floor moved aside showing the top of a step down.

A dry rotting smell came up from out of the hole.

"There is another lever here, but going to need two or three of your people lifting on that wall there as I pull it."

Three of the workers lifted as Sarge pulled the lever hidden on the trim behind the door and the piece of wall with a horrid grinding sound lifted and vanished.

"Okay," Sarge said. "Someone put some nails in those levers to hold them in place," pointing to the area behind the door.

One of the workers stepped to do as Sarge asked.

"Can we block up that wall and block the entrance open so it doesn't close up?"

Baker nodded to another of his guys and pointed to the back door and the guy went out that way.

"And we're going to need full oxygen masks to go down in there," Robin said.

Again Baker sent a worker to get them.

While they were waiting, standing above the open staircase, Pickett couldn't believe they had found this place. Granted, it was stunningly well hidden, but fifty years of looking and remodeling, someone should have found it.

"You know," Baker said, shaking his head. "I would have remodeled this entire building, including this basement and never once known that room was down there. More than likely it is as large as this entire basement."

"Got a hunch," Pickett said, "there is more than a room down there."

CHAPTER SIX

The workers got the two slabs blocked open and another fresh-air hose like the one on the staircase pumping fresh air in through the back door while fans blew out the bad air.

"Gloves," Robin said and for the first time in years Pickett put on crime scene gloves.

"We can't touch anything at this point," Sarge said. "If Becky is down there, we're going to need an active detective to come on scene and finish all this."

"You okay with this?" Pickett asked Baker and he nodded. No doubt there wasn't a chance in the world as an architect he was going to miss this, dead body or not.

Pickett glanced around to make sure the other three were masked up, then she carefully started down the stairs with her cell phone flashlight on.

It was clear that this staircase was made for regular customers, more than likely in dress clothes because it widened out almost at once.

And the room beyond was like a picture out of time. A long wooden bar filled the wall to Pickett's right, with a good twenty ornate barstools in front of it and hundreds of bottles on the back bar, most still looked full.

A good twenty ornate wooden tables surrounded by cloth chairs filled the center of the room and on the far wall was a bandstand with instruments still in their stands and an empty wooden dance floor in front of the bandstand.

The walls were covered with drapes and art and posters from the 1930s. Everything was just frozen in time.

Pickett got to the bottom of the staircase and moved to one side to let the others join her. She could hear her own breathing in her ears inside the mask. And she knew almost instantly she was feeling shock.

The shock wasn't from stepping back ninety years in time, but from the scene at two tables in front of her near the bar.

There were five mummified bodies slumped either on the table or on the floor by the table.

All of them had a glass of whiskey in front of them, and there were two bottles on the table.

One of the women was dressed in the clothes Becky Williams had last been seen in. And her hair was the right length and color.

"Looks like Becky Williams was having a party," Sarge said.

"And with tainted forty-year-old moonshine," Robin said. "Clearly that stuff killed them quickly. None of them even made a move for the door."

"I think I'm going to be sick," Baker said.

Sarge turned him and hustled him back up the staircase as fast as they could go.

"I'll call in the active detectives," Sarge said as he left.

Pickett managed to turn away from the death scene. To the right of the end of the bar was a door and Pickett and Robin moved over and opened it.

It was a storage area full of shelves and shelves of booze in bottles. And tucked off to one side, between the shelves, were two other mummified bodies. From the looks of it, they had died in the 1950s for the same reason as the ones out front. Drinking pure poison.

"Seems on our first day back not only have we solved Becky Williams's case," Robin said. "Just as we all thought, she was in the speakeasy. But now we got six others. Just got to figure out who they were."

"Yeah," Pickett said. "Won't that be fun?"

Robin laughed, but Pickett knew that with her and her husband's computer skills, she would have the six identified very quickly. At least the ones from the 1970s with Becky.

Pickett and Robin went back out into the big room frozen in time in the 1930s and stopped for a moment to take one last look at the room and the bodies slumped around the table. It was just amazing, an image of art almost, a very real representation showing how many deaths Prohibition had caused.

"Not sure I'm ever going to forget this one," Robin said.

"Yeah," Pickett said. "An amazing first day back."

"Got that right," Robin said.

Then as they turned for the staircase, Pickett asked, "Do you think there's any chance that one of those guys with Becky might be D. B. Cooper?"

Robin laughed and then said, "After all this, it wouldn't surprise me in the slightest."

Pickett also laughed. "Yeah, I agree there."

NEWSLETTER SIGN-UP

Follow Dean on BookBub

Be the first to know!

Just sign up for the Dean Wesley Smith newsletter, and keep up with the latest news, releases and so much more—even the occasional giveaway.

So, what are you waiting for? To sign up go to deanwesleysmith.com.

But wait! There's more. Sign up for the WMG Publishing newsletter, too, and get the latest news and releases from all of the WMG authors and lines, including Kristine Kathryn Rusch, Kristine Grayson, Kris Nelscott, *Pulphouse Fiction Magazine, Smith's Monthly,* and so much more.

To sign up go to wmgpublishing.com.

ABOUT THE AUTHOR

Dean Wesley Smith

Considered one of the most prolific writers working in modern fiction, *USA Today* bestselling writer Dean Wesley Smith published far more than a hundred novels in forty years, and hundreds of short stories across many genres.

At the moment he produces novels in several major series, including the time travel Thunder Mountain novels set in the Old West, the galaxy-spanning Seeders Universe series, the urban fantasy Ghost of a Chance series, a superhero series starring Poker Boy, and a mystery series featuring the retired detectives of the Cold Poker Gang.

His monthly magazine, *Smith's Monthly*, which consists of only his own fiction, premiered in October 2013 and offers readers more than 70,000 words per issue, including a new and original novel every month.

During his career, Dean also wrote a couple dozen *Star Trek* novels, the only two original *Men in Black* novels, Spider-Man and X-Men novels, plus novels set in gaming and television worlds. Writing with his wife Kristine Kathryn Rusch under the name Kathryn Wesley, he wrote the novel for the NBC miniseries The Tenth Kingdom and other books for *Hallmark Hall of Fame* movies.

He wrote novels under dozens of pen names in the worlds of comic books and movies, including novelizations of almost a dozen films, from *The Final Fantasy* to *Steel* to *Rundown*.

Dean also worked as a fiction editor off and on, starting at Pulphouse Publishing, then at *VB Tech Journal*, then Pocket Books, and now at WMG Publishing, where he and Kristine Kathryn Rusch serve as series editors for the acclaimed *Fiction River* anthology series.

For more information about Dean's books and ongoing projects, please visit his website at www.deanwesleysmith.com and sign up for his newsletter.

For more information:
www.deanwesleysmith.com

f facebook.com/deanwsmith3

|●| patreon.com/deanwesleysmith

BB bookbub.com/authors/dean-wesley-smith

www.ingramcontent.com/pod-product-compliance
Lightning Source LLC
Chambersburg PA
CBHW010516100726
47903CB00009B/2776

9 781561 468744